Merry shuddered,
pulling Douglas's coat close.

Leather, soap, subtle masculinity. They clung to the
bomber jacket and to Merry. She took a few steps away
from the activity, wanting to run back to her SUV and
drive home. Wanting to believe that the young woman's
heartbreaking death would change nothing.

Just stay calm.

Answer the questions.

Try not to look like a crimi...

But she was.

She was.

FI... ...ED BAY:

Law enforcement siblings fight for justice and family

Books by Shirlee McCoy

SHIRLEE McCOY

has always loved making up stories. As a child, she daydreamed elaborate tales in which she was the heroine—gutsy, strong and invincible. Though she soon grew out of her superhero fantasies, her love for storytelling never diminished. She knew early that she wanted to write inspirational fiction, and she began writing her first novel when she was a teenager. Still, it wasn't until her third son was born that she truly began pursuing her dream of being published. Three years later, she sold her first book. Now a busy mother of five, Shirlee is a homeschool mom by day and an inspirational author by night. She and her husband and children live in the Pacific Northwest and share their house with a dog, two cats and a bird. You can visit her website at www.shirleemccoy.com, or email her at shirlee@shirleemccoy.com.

SHIRLEE McCOY

THE LAWMAN'S LEGACY

Love Inspired

Special thanks and acknowledgment to Shirlee McCoy for her contribution to the Fitzgerald Bay miniseries.

Recycling programs for this product may not exist in your area.

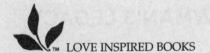

LOVE INSPIRED BOOKS

ISBN-13: 978-0-373-44473-1

THE LAWMAN'S LEGACY

Copyright © 2012 by Harlequin Books S.A.

www.LoveInspiredBooks.com

Printed in U.S.A.

Dear Reader,

Welcome to Love Inspired!

2012 is a very special year for us. It marks the fifteenth anniversary of Love Inspired Books. Hard to believe that fifteen years ago, we first began publishing our warm and wonderful inspirational romances.

Back in 1997, we offered readers three books a month. Since then we've expanded quite a bit! In addition to the heartwarming contemporary romances of Love Inspired, we have the exciting romantic suspenses of Love Inspired Suspense, and the adventurous historical romances of Love Inspired Historical. Whatever your reading preference, we've got fourteen books a month for you to choose from now!

Throughout the year we'll be celebrating in several different ways. Look for books by bestselling authors who've been writing for us since the beginning, stories by brand-new authors you won't want to miss, special miniseries in all three lines, reissues of top authors, and much, much more.

This is our way of thanking you for reading Love Inspired books. We know our uplifting stories of hope, faith and love touch your hearts as much as they touch ours.

Join us in celebrating fifteen amazing years of inspirational romance!

Blessings,

Melissa Endlich and Tina James

Senior Editors of Love Inspired Books

Ah, Sovereign Lord, you have made the heavens
and the earth by your great power and outstretched
arm. Nothing is too hard for you.
—*Jeremiah* 32:17

ONE

Captain Douglas Fitzgerald pulled up in front of his father's colonial-style house, eyeing the line of cars that stretched along the curb. The entire Fitzgerald clan had gathered for his grandfather's birthday celebration, and it looked like he was the last to arrive. Not a problem. He had a foolproof excuse. Duty first. That's the way his father had raised him. It was the only way he knew how to be. Seeing as how he was working his shift with the Fitzgerald Bay police department, he had no choice but to show up late and leave early. His father knew that. His grandfather knew it.

Yeah. He had an excuse, but he still wished he could spend a little more time visiting with Granddad and the rest of the clan and a little less time doing paperwork back at the office. He loved Fitzgerald Bay. Loved the people, the community, the easy predictability of small-town life, but predictability could be boring.

Or, maybe, it was just his life that could be boring.

Routine.

Predictable.

Empty?

He frowned as he stepped into the oversize foyer.

Voices carried from the dining room, the sound of

σ

laughter and chatter ringing through his childhood home
Empty? His life had never been that. Could never be that
Not with his boisterous family around.

But there *were* moments when he felt that something
was missing.

Some*one* was missing.

He frowned again.

No one was missing. Nothing was missing. His life wa
exactly the way he wanted it to be.

"Douglas!" His sister Keira smiled as he walked into
the foyer. Still dressed in her police uniform, straight dark
hair pulled into a ponytail, her cheeks pink, she looked
closer to sixteen than twenty-three.

"I can't stay long. Looks like everyone is having a good
time." He glanced at the throng of family members.

"Did you expect anything less?"

"Not when it comes to our family. Where's Granddad?

"Holding court in the living room. You'd better go se
him. He's been asking when you were going to get here."

"He knew I had to work."

"He's still been asking." She shrugged.

"I'll go see what he wants." Douglas walked into the
large, comfortable living room, waved to his grandfather

"You finally made it." Ian Fitzgerald stood as Dougla
approached. Tall and handsome, he'd only recently begun
to slow down, the years finally starting to catch with
him.

"What did you need to see me about?"

"Not you. Everyone. I have an announcement to make
and I didn't want to make it before you got here. Can
have everyone's attention?" He raised his voice, the boom
ing sound quieting the laughter and chatter. Several peopl
stepped into the room and waited while Ian cleared hi
throat, looked around at his family.

Douglas's family. Cousins. Uncles. Aunts. His brothers Ryan, Owen and Charles. His sisters Fiona and Keira. His father, frowning as he waited for Ian to continue.

"What is it, Dad?" Aiden Fitzgerald asked. Chief of the Fitzgerald Bay police department, Douglas's father wore authority like a mantle, his shoulders straight, his carriage upright.

"I've been doing a lot of thinking lately. Thirty years is a long time to be mayor, and it's time to step down, let someone else take my place."

"You're not going to run for mayor this term?" Douglas spoke over the shocked reaction of the entire Fitzgerald clan.

"I'm not. So, are we going to have cake?" Ian settled back into the chair, crossing his arms over his chest. He'd made up his mind. That much was obvious. Douglas was certain he wouldn't change it. Not Granddad.

"Cake? Dad, you can't just drop a bomb like that and expect us to move on," Aiden responded.

"Bomb? I'm eighty-two, Aiden. I can't keep going forever. I think we all know that. It's time to slow down. To enjoy the family God gave me while I still have the time and health to do it. Seems to me, you're about the age I was when I ran for mayor the first time. It's your turn to run this town."

"I'm the chief of police. I can't be mayor, too."

"You've got three sons you're training to take your place. Might as well let one of them have a go at being chief."

The two could debate the issue all day. Douglas had no doubt about that. He'd let them and check in later to see if his father had talked Granddad into backing down. For now, he needed to eat and get back to work.

"You two work things out. I'm going to—" Before he

could finish, Douglas's radio crackled, and Deborah Sandino's voice carried across the line.

"Captain? We have a situation on our hands." The hint of panic in her words made Douglas's heart jump. Deborah had been a dispatcher with the police department for over a decade, and Douglas had never known her to be anything but calm and efficient.

"What kind of situation?" He met his father's eyes, the sudden silence of the room making Deborah's words echo loudly.

"A body has been found near the lighthouse."

"Where?"

"At the base of the cliffs. The caller believes the deceased may be Olivia Henry."

"It can't be Olivia." Douglas's brother Charles spoke into the deafening silence that followed Deborah's announcement, his face drawn with concern. Divorced and the custodial parent to his twin toddlers, he'd hired Olivia to work as their nanny several months ago. Sweet and kindhearted, she'd poured out love on her charges, and that had been enough to win the respect and affection of the family.

Now she might be dead, her body lying broken at the base of the lighthouse cliffs.

"I'll be at the scene in ten minutes, Deborah. No one is to touch the body before I get there." He jogged through the living room and back out into the frigid afternoon. Steel gray clouds blocked the sun and the air held a hint of snow. A winter storm blowing in. They'd need to collect evidence and retrieve the body before it arrived.

The body?

The young woman.

The human being whose life had ended abruptly.

An accident?

A suicide?

Something worse?

"Hold up, son. I'm riding with you," Aiden called out, pulling on a thick coat as he ran to Douglas's SUV. Face pale, his hands trembling, he looked shaken and ill.

"You don't have to—"

"I'm the chief of police. Of course I have to." He jumped into the SUV, and Douglas gunned the engine, sped through town, sirens blaring, lights flashing, adrenaline pumping through his blood. A quiet fishing community, Fitzgerald Bay didn't offer much in the way of excitement for its police force. Loitering, vandalism and robbery topped the list of crimes. Every once in a while, domestic violence or assault, but bodies didn't appear at the base of cliffs. People didn't just die without warning and without cause.

Someone *had* died, though.

Maybe someone very close to his family.

Douglas's hands tightened on the steering wheel, his heart thundering in time with his racing thoughts.

"Do you think it's Olivia?" Aiden asked, his voice shaky and weak.

"I don't know." Douglas glanced at his father, worried about him in a way he'd never been before. Aiden had served as chief of police for as many years as Douglas could remember. Stoic, serious and unflappable, he wasn't the kind of guy to let anything shake him. But he was shaken. Visibly so. "Are you okay, Dad?"

"Of course I am," Aiden muttered as Douglas flew down Main Street and out onto the rural road that led to the bluff and the lighthouse. Two police cars followed, lights flashing blue and red through the cloudy afternoon. His brothers. Douglas was sure of it. No way would Ryan or Owen stay away. No doubt, Keira was in one of the cars.

Together, they'd identify the body. They'd piece together what happened.

He just hoped they wouldn't find Olivia.

Hoped she was happily enjoying her day off.

The lighthouse loomed in the distance, growing closer with every passing mile. White and red, it stood stark and tall against the steely sky. A small, quaint cottage was a few dozen yards away from it. Once the lighthouse keeper's home, it now belonged to Charles. He'd built a small apartment at the back of the building and had offered it to Olivia.

Maybe, she was there.

Douglas *prayed* she was there.

Charles's blue Nissan, the one Olivia used to transport the twins, and a beat-up Chevy station wagon sat in the driveway. Dark green. Wood trim. Looked like it had lived a few decades too long.

Douglas knew the car, had seen it parked outside his sister Fiona's bookstore dozens of times in the past year. He knew exactly who it belonged to. Remembered the day he'd walked into the Reading Nook and seen Meredith O'Leary for the first time. Curvy, pretty, *secretive* Merry.

Had she found the body?

"That's Merry's car," Aiden said as Douglas got out of the SUV. Gulls screamed, their haunting cries mixing with crashing waves as Douglas made his way along the path to the cliff.

Large boulders and smaller rocks jutted from dark soil. The briny scent of the bay carried on the cold wind that blew across the bluff. All of it felt familiar and homey and right, but nothing was right about the day or Douglas's reason for being at the lighthouse.

Up ahead, a woman stood near the edge of the cliff,

strawberry blond hair whipping in the wind, shoulders hunched against the cold.

Definitely Merry.

There was no mistaking her hair, her ultra-feminine curves, or the way his stomach clenched, his senses springing to life when he saw her.

Two lunch dates. That's all it had taken to convince him that Merry was a woman worth knowing better. He'd looked into her eyes, listened to her laughter and imagined doing the same over and over again in the weeks and years to come.

Two dates.

And, then she'd broken things off.

It's just not working out.

That's what she'd said, but she'd refused to look in his eyes when she'd said it, refused to tell him what part of their time together hadn't worked for her.

Because it had all worked for him.

She stepped closer to the cliff's unstable edge, and his heart lurched.

"Merry!" he called out, but she didn't seem to hear over the crashing waves and screaming gulls. He ran forward and snagged her coat, yanking her away from the crumbling earth before it could give way.

She screamed, turning around, her fist aiming for his nose and coming a little too close for comfort.

"Hey, calm down!" He sidestepped another blow, grabbing her hands before she could swing again. They trembled in his grip, the fine tremors making Douglas ease his grip, smooth the skin of her knuckles.

"Douglas! Thank goodness you're here. Olivia is..." Her voice trailed off as if she couldn't bear to speak the words, and he had no doubt she really believed Olivia was lying at the base of the cliffs. But it was a hundred feet down to the rocks and water. A hundred feet could make identifying someone difficult.

"Stay here. I'll take a look."

Please, God, don't let it be her.

The prayer whispered through his mind as he approached the cliff edge, looked below at the rocks and crashing waves.

A body sprawled facedown on slick rock. Arms and legs splayed. Blond hair soaked and trailing into foamy puddles. Even from a distance, Douglas recognized the small frame and delicate line of the neck.

Olivia.

For sure.

Dead.

For sure.

His father stepped up beside him, tensing as he looked at Olivia's body. "It's her."

"Yeah. I'm afraid so."

"We need to be the first to examine the body. If she fell, fine. If she didn't, we need to know what happened. I'll get the climbing gear." Aiden hurried away, not giving Douglas time to respond.

If she fell.

The words seemed to hang in the air. The other possibilities hovering with them.

If she hadn't fallen...

"We were supposed to meet for lunch," Merry said, and Douglas wasn't sure if she was speaking to him or to herself.

He turned, studying her pale, pretty face, searching her dark, hollow eyes. Haunted. That's how she looked. How she *always* looked. Despite her smile, despite her easy laughter, there were always shadows in her eyes. He'd noticed them before he'd asked her to lunch, had wanted to find out what caused them, but Merry had shut him out. "Were you here looking for her?"

"Yes. She was late, and she didn't answer her phone. I got worried and came to make sure she was okay. I thought maybe she'd overslept or her car hadn't started. I never thought…" She shook her head.

"You went to her apartment first?"

"Yes. The door was unlocked, and I walked inside. Checked her bedroom. She wasn't there. She loves the bluff and looking out over the bay. I thought maybe she'd come here and lost track of time, so I came to check. I don't know what made me look down. Maybe just a feeling that things weren't right. Do you think she fell?"

"I won't know until I get down there. For now, I'm going to assume that's what happened. Unless you know something that makes you think differently."

She hesitated, her dark gaze skittering away. "I don't."

Lying?

Maybe. Or maybe she was still in shock, still trying to wrap her mind around Olivia's death. He couldn't blame her if she was. He couldn't wrap his mind around it. He'd seen Olivia the previous day, pushing Charles's twins in a double stroller, a smile on her face.

He shoved the image away.

He needed to focus on the job. There'd be time to mourn later.

He scanned the ground near the cliff, looking for signs of a struggle, some clue that would help put together a picture of what had happened. No footprints, but a few feet away, the earth seemed scuffed. Nearby, a black shoe lay near a clump of winter-brown foliage, and he crouched nearby. Woman's sneaker with green shoelaces.

"It's Olivia's." Merry crouched beside him, reached out.

He snagged her hand before she could grab the sneaker, felt the tension beneath smooth skin.

"We need to leave it for the evidence team."

"Evidence of what?" she asked, tugging her hand away and tucking it into the pocket of her coat. Her cheeks were red from cold, her breath coming out in quick puffs that hung in the icy air.

"Of whatever happened here."

"You ready to go down, Douglas?" Douglas's older brother, Ryan, approached, climbing gear flung over his shoulder, his face hard. Deputy chief of police, he'd earned his title through hard work and commitment to the job. Keira and Owen were right behind him, Aiden taking up the rear. Every Fitzgerald police officer was in attendance, but there was nothing they could do for Olivia. Nothing but recover her body, notify her next of kin and see that she had a proper burial.

"I'm ready." He slid into the gear as Merry watched, her body so tense and tight he thought she might break.

"Why don't you wait near your car, Merry? I have a few questions I'd like to ask when I'm finished here."

"Sure." She seemed relieved by his suggestion, happy to be allowed to leave the cliff. He watched as she ran toward the cottage, her hair flying wild behind her.

"She seems upset," Keira said.

"She and Olivia were pretty chummy, so that's not surprising," Ryan responded as he helped Douglas hook into the harness. "Ready, bro?"

"Ready."

"Take the camera down with you. The way those waves are crashing, we could lose evidence quickly." His brother Owen, a detective with the police department, handed him a camera, and Douglas tucked it into his pocket.

"Will do." Icy spray seeped through his uniform as he rappelled down the slick rock.

Olivia's body lay a few feet away, water lapping at her hand and seeping over the surface of the boulder under her. He snapped photos quickly, gulls screaming overhead as he worked, his mind separating fact from emotion.

Olivia. Living, breathing, laughing Olivia.

Dead.

It was his job to chronicle the scene. Make sure nothing was missed. He couldn't let sorrow cloud his vision or his objectivity.

Blood stained the blond hair at the back of Olivia's skull, and he snapped a picture.

Bruised cheek.

Snap.

Arms and legs splayed.

Snap.

Bruises on one wrist that might have been finger marks.

Snap.

He frowned, studying the angle of Olivia's head and neck. She lay facedown, but the wound was to the back of her head, the skin behind her ear broken. A deadly blow, for sure. He snapped a close-up of the wound and glanced up, trying to imagine a way that she might have fallen and slammed the back of her head into the face of the cliff. Pounding waves had carved a shallow hollow beneath the bluff, and it would have been difficult for anyone to fall into the rock wall. Didn't mean it hadn't happened, though.

He snapped a photo of the cliff's edge. Snapped another of the scene, Olivia's splayed body on dark gray rock. Nothing else but a fist-size rock that lay a foot from the remains. He crouched next to it, used his flashlight to turn the heavy stone. A few long strands of blond hair clung to it, glued on by dark clotted blood.

And he knew what he was dealing with.
Not a horrible tragic accident.
A murder.

TWO

Kindhearted, sweet Olivia. Gone.

It didn't seem possible.

Couldn't be true.

But no matter how much she wanted to wipe the image out of her mind, Merry couldn't shake the picture of Olivia's body lying lifeless as waves crashed just feet away. She rubbed her arms, but there was no easing the icy chill that had settled in her heart.

Sadness.

Anxiety.

Fear.

Heart-pounding, breath-stealing fear.

Her blood flowed cold with it, and she couldn't shake that. No matter how hard she tried.

Police milled around the lighthouse grounds searching for clues that would help them figure out how Olivia had ended up at the base of the cliff. All Merry could do was stand still, stay quiet, pray that she didn't call any undue attention to herself.

"Merry? Are you okay?" Keira Fitzgerald hurried toward her, black hair gleaming in the hazy sunlight. The youngest of the Fitzgerald police officers, Keira was the least intimidating of the group, but she was still an officer of the law. Not someone Merry wanted to spend more than a few minutes talking to. Better to talk to her than Douglas, though. Douglas who tempted Merry in a way no man ever had. Tempted her to say things she shouldn't, believe in things she shouldn't. She should never have agreed to have lunch with him once, let alone twice. But she had. She'd sat across the table from him, looked into his blue eyes and known how dangerous a game she was playing. Two shared meals, and she'd wanted to confess everything. So, she'd told him what she had to, that things weren't working out, and she'd done her best to avoid him ever since.

"*Are* you okay?" Keira repeated, and she nodded.

"Fine. I just wish Olivia was, too." Her voice broke, and she swallowed back tears.

"You and Olivia were close, weren't you?"

"We were friends."

"You were going to meet her for lunch?" Keira scribbled something in a small notebook, and Merry nodded.

"She had the day off, and my landlady offered to watch Tyler. We thought it would be the perfect opportunity to spend some time together without kids. Not that Olivia didn't like being with the twins. She did, but..." She pressed her lips together, forced back the avalanche of words.

Short, simple, to the point. That's what she needed to be when it came to dealing with the police.

"When was the last time you spoke to her?"

"Yesterday afternoon when we confirmed our plans."

"Did you notice anything unusual during your conversation?"

"No."

"She didn't seem upset? Worried? Anxious?" Keira pressed, and the words shivered along Merry's spine. Too many questions being asked about the tragedy, and there had to be a reason.

"No. Why?"

"What time did you arrive at the lighthouse?" Keira sidestepped the question.

"Twelve-thirty."

"Did you see anything out of the ordinary?"

"What's going on, Keira?"

"Look, we don't want this spread around yet, but it looks like Olivia didn't fall. The evidence suggests she was dead or unconscious before she hit the rocks."

"She was murdered?" Merry's heart jumped, her stomach churning.

"That's what the evidence is pointing to."

"Who would do such a thing?"

"That's what we're hoping you can help us with. Olivia arrived in town three months ago. Now she's dead. Probably murdered. She brought some kind of trouble with her. That's what we're thinking. You were her closest friend in town. Maybe you know what that trouble was."

"Like you said, she's only been in town for a few months. It's hard to get close to someone in such a short amount of time." She took a deep breath, trying to calm her racing pulse. Stick as close to the truth as possible. Give the police as much information as she could. Go home and pray that she wouldn't be pulled any further into the investigation. That was the plan. All she had to do was stick to it, and she'd be fine. Tyler would be fine.

Please, God, let him be fine.

"Funny, Fiona has mentioned you and Olivia getting together on a fair number of occasions. You don't consider that close?"

"I liked Olivia. She was very sweet and easy to get along with, but we hung out together because we were both new to town ˺d we both had young children with us all the time. We ˺idn't share much about our lives outside of work and kids." Not much, but they had shared some. At least, Olivia had.

More secrets.

Too many secrets.

"I see." Keira scribbled something else into the notebook, and Merry was tempted to yank it from her hand, read what she'd written.

"I wish I could tell you more, Keira. I really do."

"Did Olivia mention any—"

"Have they brought up her body yet?" Dr. Charles Fitzgerald interrupted as he walked toward them, his expression grim, his eyes dark with sadness. Though he'd treated Tyler for ear infections several times in the past year, Merry didn't know him well. Olivia had spoken highly of him though. Called him a gentleman, a great father and a wonderful employer.

"Not yet. It should be soon, though. You know you're not going to be able to examine her body, right? That's going to have to be left to the medical examiner," Keira responded.

"I know, but I need to be here anyway. She was the kids' nanny. She loved them, and they loved her."

"Was she in her apartment when you left this morning?" Keira asked, all her attention on her brother.

Good.

Maybe Merry could get in her car, drive home to her son. Hide away until everything blew over.

Only she didn't think this was going to blow over.

There would be questions. Lots of them.

And, that could mean trouble.

Merry moved away from the siblings, their conversation swirling on cold January air and following her as she walked to the edge of the path that led to the cliff. She didn't want to go back, didn't want to see Olivia's body pulled up from the rocks, but she had to.

Three months wasn't a long time to be friends, but it had been enough time to know that Olivia was alone. A transplant from Ireland, she had a cousin in the States, but no other family close by. Someone had to stand vigil as her body was retrieved. Since Charles was being interviewed, Merry was the only one left.

She followed the path, bypassing the lighthouse and winding her way toward the cliff's edge. Gulls screamed, their banshee cries piercing the air. She shivered, pulling her coat tight against cold wind as she ducked under the tape.

"The tape is there for a reason." The deep baritone cut through her thoughts, pulled her back to the present and the problem at hand. Douglas Fitzgerald blocked her path, his broad, muscular chest at eye level.

She had to look up to meet his gaze.

Way up.

"Someone needs to be there when Olivia is brought up. She doesn't have family around, so…" Her voice trailed off as he studied her face, his eyes so intensely blue that she wanted to look away. She was sure he could read her secrets, see all the things she'd spent four years keeping hidden.

That was why things hadn't worked out.

That was why two dates had been two too many.

That was why she avoided the man like the plague.

Only she couldn't avoid him now, couldn't turn and run in the other direction.

"So, you thought you would be her family and keep watch over her? I wish I could let you, but this is a crime scene." His words were gentle, his touch light as he urged her back under the tape.

"I won't touch anything. I just want to…" What did she want to do? Pray for Olivia's family? Make sure her friend's remains were treated with respect?

"My family cared about Olivia, too, Merry. I promise you, we'll make sure she's treated with dignity."

"Olivia has a cousin in the States. You're going to have to call her."

"Do you have a name or contact information?"

"Meghan, maybe? I'm not a hundred percent sure." She wasn't a hundred percent sure of much when it came to Olivia. A half-dozen years her junior, Olivia had been as closemouthed and protective of her past as Merry. That had seemed to suit them both fine. Maybe it was one of the main reasons they'd become friends. Neither asked many questions. Neither gave a lot of answers.

Only, now, Olivia was dead and there was no way to avoid questions or answers.

Please, God, let the questions just be about Olivia. Not about me, or my life, or Tyler.

She shivered, and Douglas rubbed her arms, the quick, brusque touch doing nothing to warm her. Her teeth chattered, and she dragged the coat tighter around her chest. She wanted to zip it, but her hands were shaking violently, and she was afraid Douglas would notice.

"You're cold," he said in the same gentle tone he'd used before, and she knew why every unattached woman in Fitzgerald Bay wanted to capture Douglas's attention. Knew why the women at church whispered as he settled into the pew with the rest of the Fitzgeralds. Knew exactly why she'd agreed to go to lunch with him twice and why it was absolutely imperative that she never do such a foolish thing again. His tone, his eyes, they begged confidence.

promised protection, made a woman want to trust him with all her worries and every one of her deepest darkest secrets.

"I'm okay."

"You're freezing." He grabbed the hem of her coat, had it zipped before she realized what he was doing. "Why don't you go home and warm up? I'll stop by your place and interview you after I finish here."

Stop by her place?

Be near Tyler?

No.

Never.

Not in a million years.

That's what she wanted to say, but couldn't.

"I don't mind waiting here until you're finished."

"It could take hours, and the wind is picking up, the temperature is dropping. Charles's place is off-limits until we finish dusting for prints, and you'll either have to sit in your car or stand out in the cold. Go on home. I'll meet you there as soon as I can." He turned away, assuming that she'd go along with his plan. She wanted to. She really did. But she couldn't risk having him so close to Tyler.

"I'll be warm enough waiting in my car, and that will save you the effort of driving over to my place."

"Is there some reason why you don't want me to stop by your house?" He scanned her face, searching for the things she held close to her heart, the truths she'd never dared tell anyone.

"Of course not. I just thought that if I waited here, I'd save you some time," she lied, because she couldn't tell him how much the thought of having a police officer near her son terrified her.

"If you want to save me time, stop arguing about where

I'm going to interview you and go home," he said with a half smile that made her heart flutter.

Foolish heart.

Even terror couldn't keep it from reacting when Douglas was around. She *had* to keep her distance. Had to keep him out of her house, out of her life, *out of her heart*.

Above all, she had to keep him away from Tyler.

"Interview me about what? I've already told you what I know." Even she could hear the desperation in her tone, and Douglas didn't miss it. His gaze sharpened, and he stepped close, his expression taut and hard as he cupped her shoulders and looked down into her face.

"What are you hiding, Merry?"

"Nothing."

"Then why are you so nervous?"

"Because Olivia is gone. Murdered, and I don't know why. I can't believe anyone would want to hurt her," she responded truthfully, hoping it would be enough to assuage Douglas.

"Someone did hurt her though, and I'm hoping you can help us figure out who that was. That's why I need to interview you."

"I didn't know her very well. Not well enough to tell you anything that could help."

"You may be surprised at what you know and how much it helps. So, how about we stop arguing about this, and you go on home?" he asked, but it wasn't a suggestion. He expected her to comply, and she knew she didn't have a choice.

"We weren't arguing. We were discussing." She walked back to her car, giving up the fight to keep him away from her house. She'd just have to keep the interview focused on Olivia, keep it away from *her* past, *her* son, *her* secrets.

Douglas kept pace beside her, his silence grating her

nerves and making her want to speak into it, offer more explanations for her reluctance, try to convince him that she had nothing to hide.

Because she didn't.

Not anything that had to do with Olivia, anyway.

Several officers stood outside the door that led into Olivia's tiny apartment in the cottage. Just a few hundred square feet, it consisted of a small living room, a kitchenette, a bathroom and a bedroom. Nothing fancy, but Olivia had made it homey and comfortable. Still, Merry had only visited once, Tyler's rambunctious and busy nature making it difficult to relax in the confined area.

Visited once, but she'd walked through the apartment less than an hour ago. Touched the door handles, fingered the teacup that sat at the small kitchen table. Left prints everywhere.

The thought sent ice racing through her blood.

"What are they doing?" She gestured to Keira and another officer. Both were bent over the apartment door handle.

"Dusting for prints," Douglas responded as he opened the station wagon's door.

She didn't get in. Terror froze her in place. "But Olivia died at the cliffs."

"We don't know where she died. We only know where she was found."

"I hadn't thought about that."

"Why would you?"

Good question. One she couldn't answer, because she was too busy watching Keira dust the doorknob and door frame. Too busy wishing she could run over and wipe away the dusting powder, wipe off any prints she'd left. Wipe away the traces of who she'd once been.

Please, God, don't let them find any of my fingerprints. Please.

But they would.

How could they not?

She swayed, and Douglas grabbed her arm. "Are you okay?"

"I'm fine. This is all just upsetting."

"Sit down. You're pale as paper." He urged her into the car, leaned in so they were eye to eye. "Are you going to be okay to drive home, or should I ask someone to take you?"

"I'll be okay." But her voice shook and tears she'd been denying since she'd seen Olivia lying at the base of the cliff spilled out.

"Will you?" He brushed a tear from her cheek, and she wanted to jerk away from the warmth of his palm, look away from the compassion in his eyes.

Dangerous.

So, dangerous to let him into her life.

"Of course I will be." She wiped away more tears, shoved the key into the ignition and started the engine. She *had* to be okay. Tyler was depending on her.

Douglas studied her for a moment, then nodded. "I'll see you in a couple of hours."

He closed the door and walked away, but the feel of his palm on her cheek lingered as she drove toward home, offering her a glimpse of what might have been if she hadn't had to push Douglas away.

Comfort.

Security.

Someone to lean on.

She wanted those things desperately, but she wanted the life she'd created more.

She had to remember that. Had to get a handle on her

emotions before Douglas's interview. If she didn't, she might give away too much of herself.

Four years, and she'd been fine.

Four years, and she'd kept Tyler safe.

She'd do the same for another four years and another and another.

She *would*.

All she had to do was keep her head on straight, focus on answering Douglas's questions about Olivia without giving away anything about herself or Tyler.

All she had to do was continue to keep her secrets.

Only hers weren't the only secrets she carried.

She had Olivia's secrets, too.

Keep this for me, Merry. Don't tell anyone you have it.

The words whispered through Merry's mind, as clear as they'd been the day Olivia had spoken them, her lilting Irish accent charming and warm. They mixed with other words, another time, another place, another accent. Thick Bostonian. The same as the one Merry had worked so hard to rid herself of.

Keep him safe. Please, promise me that no matter what happens, you'll keep him safe. Promise me.

So many promises, so many secrets.

Too many secrets.

And, Douglas Fitzgerald coming over to her house to ask questions.

Douglas with his winning smile and caring nature.

Douglas, who had taken her to lunch, looked deep into her eyes and made her feel beautiful and special and cared for. She couldn't stomach lying to him, but she couldn't ever tell him the truth.

Please, God, don't let him ask me questions I can't answer.

But Douglas would.

He had a reputation for fairness and honesty and dogged determination, and he had a way of looking at people and into them that made Merry nervous.

He would know she had secrets.

He probably already knew.

If he thought those secrets had anything to do with Olivia's death, he'd dig until he knew everything. Every secret. Every lie. Every bit of what Merry had kept hidden.

He'd dig until he destroyed everything she'd worked so hard to protect.

Hot tears rolled down her cheeks, and, this time, she didn't bother wiping them away.

THREE

Forty years.

That's how long it had been since someone had been murdered in Fitzgerald Bay.

Scratch that.

It had been *twelve hours* since someone had been murdered in Fitzgerald Bay. At least, that was the coroner's assessment, but Douglas hoped he was wrong. His brother Charles had a foolproof alibi for the morning. He'd left his house at eight, been at their father's place by eight-fifteen. The entire Fitzgerald clan and a few friends had seen him there.

A good alibi for the wrong time.

Which wasn't a good alibi at all.

That worried Douglas. Not because he suspected his brother, but because other people might.

A divorced doctor with a pretty young woman living in an apartment attached to his house had given the gossip mongers plenty to talk about. Would romance bloom between the divorced doctor and the Irish nanny? Would they marry and live happily ever after?

Douglas had laughed at the whispered speculations.

He wasn't laughing now.

As much as he loved the townspeople, he knew that

they'd find plenty more to whisper about now that Olivia was gone. Had Charles murdered Olivia in a fit of rage because she'd rejected him? Had there been a lover's spat? Had the handsome doctor killed the woman who cared for his children?

Olivia had been young and sweet and, seemingly, vulnerable. Where she'd lived, where she'd died, those things were circumstantial evidence that could make people eye Charles with suspicion.

Douglas couldn't let that happen.

Charles had been through a lot, and it was time for him to have a little peace. Hopefully, Douglas's visit with Merry would provide evidence, something, that would keep people from whispering and speculating. Evidence that would lead to a killer. That's what Douglas needed, and it's what he planned to find.

He pulled up in front of Merry's house, eyeing the small yellow Cape Cod. White shutters. Small porch. Toys littering the front yard. Nothing unusual about that, but there'd been something in her eyes when she'd seen Keira dusting for prints. Not just grief. Fear. Stark and dark and shimmering in the depth of her chocolate brown eyes.

He opened the gate, walked into the yard. She'd cleaned things up in the year that she'd lived in the house. Cut back shrubs and trimmed the old crab apple tree. Painted the siding and trim.

Made the little house into a warm and cozy home.

But as far as Douglas knew, she never had anyone over to visit. No church socials hosted at the O'Leary place. No playgroups with mothers and kids hanging out in the little yard. Maybe she'd had Olivia over once or twice, but that seemed to be the extent of Merry's desire to play hostess. As a matter of fact, she'd announced that things weren't working out between them a few minutes after Douglas had suggested he pick her and Tyler up after work and take them for an evening picnic in the park.

Merry had seemed truly horrified by the idea.

Just as she'd seemed horrified by the idea of Douglas stopping by her place to conduct the interview.

Too bad.

He was about to step into her world, whether she liked it or not.

He knocked on the door. Waited. Knocked again.

The door swung open. No strawberry-haired, soft-eyed woman, though. Instead, a dark-haired, black-eyed little boy looked up at him, his deeply tanned skin flushed with excitement.

"You the police?"

"I am, but you should have asked who I was before you opened the door, pal."

"I'm not Pal. I'm Tyler."

"Tyler William O'Leary! What have I told you about opening the door without permission?" Merry appeared behind her son, her eyes red-rimmed and hollow, her curls pulled up in a high ponytail.

"Not to." Tyler shifted from foot to foot, nearly bouncing with energy.

"Then why did you?"

"I saw him out the window, Mommy. He has a cool car. Just like mine. Look." Tyler held up a toy SUV.

"It doesn't matter what his car looks like, you shouldn't have opened the door. Go to your room. I want you to spend some time thinking about what you've done."

"I already thought about it, Mo—"

"Go." She pointed at a steep staircase to the right of the door, and Tyler dragged his feet as he slowly walked toward it, his gaze still on Douglas.

"Quickly, young man, or you won't get any of the cookies we made."

He shot up the stairs after that, racing to the landing and disappearing into a room.

"He's a cute kid," Douglas said, more to break the sudden silence than for anything else.

"He is, but he's a little too smart for his own good." She brushed what looked like cocoa off her apron. Faded jeans cupped round hips and long legs, and a pink sweater hugged her curves. As always, she looked pretty and soft and very, very lovely.

She also looked scared. Worried. Nervous.

"He's four, right?"

"Yes. Next year, he'll be in kindergarten but for now, he just goes to preschool three days a week. Mrs. Sanderson next door has him if I'm working the other two days. He runs her ragged. He's just so busy, and I'm worried about what will happen when he goes to school. I'm sure…" She blushed. "Sorry. You're here to talk about Olivia. Not Tyler. I tend to talk too much when I'm nervous."

"What is there to be nervous about?" he asked, and she hesitated, her dark gaze skittering away.

"Olivia is dead. You said she was probably murdered. Her murderer is still on the loose. Shouldn't I be nervous?"

Maybe, but not as nervous as she looked.

"More so if you know something about why she was killed."

"I don't, but I'm sure you have a lot of questions to ask, anyway. I have coffee going and homemade double-chocolate cookies if you'd like some. Why don't we go in the kitchen to talk?"

She led him into a small kitchen, and he inhaled chocolate and sugar and a subtle berry scent that he thought might be Merry's perfume.

He tried to ignore it as he sat at a round Formica table, but the berry scent was as difficult to ignore as the person wearing it.

As *impossible* to ignore.

He'd been on a year-long hiatus from dating when he'd seen Merry for the first time. Tired of being set up with friends of friends of friends, tired of searching for a woman who would complete him the way his mother had completed his father, tired of the games and the stress that went with every relationship he'd been in.

Tired of it all until he'd looked into Merry's face, seen her smile. He'd tried to ignore her, because he hadn't wanted all those things again. The games. The stress.

But ignoring her had been impossible and one lunch together had led to another and would have led to more if she'd let it.

She hadn't, and maybe that was what her nerves and her tension were about.

"Would you rather someone else conduct the interview?" he asked as she set a plate of cookies on the table.

"Why would I?"

"Because we're not strangers? Because we were heading toward being more than friends?"

"We went to lunch together. It's not a big deal."

"Not to me, but you seem bothered by the fact that I'm here. I thought maybe that was why." He grabbed a cookie and bit into it, waiting for her response.

It came slowly.

Very slowly.

Maybe even *too* slowly.

She walked to the counter, grabbed a mug from a cupboard and poured coffee into it, her hands shaking so hard liquid sloshed over her hand.

"I'm not bothered by the fact that you're here. It's just

been a tough day, and I'm…upset." She handed him the mug, their fingers touching, heat arching between them, quicksilver and bright. He couldn't ignore *that,* either.

He grabbed her hand before she moved away, his thumb running over the rapid pulse in her wrist. "You're not just upset. You're nervous. If I'm not causing that, then what is?"

"Everything." She glanced at the doorway as if she expected someone to walk in and rescue her.

"Care to explain?"

"You're here to ask me questions about Olivia. What do you want to know?"

"You're avoiding my question."

"Because I don't want to explain." She sat down across from him, grabbed a cookie from the plate.

He could keep pushing against a wall of resistance, or he could change tactics and come at things from a different angle, see if that would give him the answers he wanted.

"You've known Olivia for five months?" he asked, and she frowned.

"You know she's only been in town for three months."

"Right. I just wondered if you did. Where did you two meet?" He knew the answer to that, too, but the benign questions were doing exactly what he intended.

Merry relaxed, the tension in her face easing.

"We talked for a few minutes after story time at the Reading Nook. A few days later, we saw each other at church. She was a really nice girl. Very easy to spend time with." She smiled sadly, and the sorrow Douglas had been tamping down since he'd stood over Olivia's broken body reared up. Made his gut clench and his chest tighten. She'd been too young to die, too sweet to be killed so brutally.

"She was. I know Charles appreciated how good she was with the twins." He kept his voice steady and his tone light. He needed to push the interview forward, not dwell in the emotions of the day.

"She was great with them. She'd have made a wonderful mother." Merry swallowed hard and stood again, pacing across the room to stare out a window above the sink.

"How did she seem in the last few days? Happy? Upset? Anxious?"

"She was just her normal self."

"So, she didn't mention anything that was bothering her? Didn't seem to have anything on her mind?" He asked the same question in a different way, hoping for a different answer. Wanting a different answer. They needed something to go on if they were going to find Olivia's murderer.

Merry stiffened but didn't turn from the window. "She didn't mention anything that was bothering her."

"Then what *did* she mention?"

"Nothing," she responded too quickly, her voice tight. If he'd been looking in her eyes, he'd have seen the lie. He knew it, and he wanted to know what she was lying about.

"You're a poor liar."

"I'm not—"

"Save us both some time, okay? Don't deny it. Olivia said something to you. What was it?"

"It was private. I don't think she wanted me to share it," Merry hedged, and he put a hand on her shoulder, urged her around so he could look into her face.

"Olivia is dead, Merry. Murdered. Keeping a secret for her can't change that."

"I know…it's just…" She bit her lip.

"What?"

"She made me promise not to mention it to anyone."

A promise, huh?

That might mean something important.

"I don't think she would expect you to keep your promise under the circumstances."

"Maybe not, and it really wasn't a big deal. At least, it didn't seem like one. Last week, Olivia brought the twins over. While she was here, she said her sweetheart might come looking for her one day. She'd never mentioned a sweetheart before, so it stuck in my mind."

"A boyfriend?" His pulse jumped at the news. He'd needed a lead. It looked like he just might have one.

"I guess so, but she didn't use that term. She just said, 'sweetheart.'"

"And, you didn't ask who her sweetheart was? Where he was?"

"Tyler spilled his juice, and I had to clean it up. By the time I finished, the moment had passed." She shrugged, and he could almost feel her forcing each muscle to relax. The tension was still in her face though, the lie still in her eyes.

What was she hiding?

Why was she hiding it?

"There's more, and I need you to tell me what it is."

"I already told you everything she told me." But there was something in her voice that said different. Something that edged along Douglas's nerves, made him study her pale face a little more intently.

"I don't believe you."

"What you believe doesn't matter. What matters is the truth, and the truth is I've told you everything Olivia said."

"Then, what aren't you telling me?"

"Just that I'm exhausted, and I'm ready for this interview to be over." She offered a half smile, and he had to admit, she looked tired. Dark circles beneath her eyes, pale skin.

"Late night?"

"Nightmares," she responded, and then frowned, picking at a chipped spot on the tile countertop.

"I'd think tonight would be the night for that."

"It probably will be. I don't think I'll ever forget looking down and…" She shook her head and didn't continue.

"It's tough. Really tough. But I have to keep asking questions, Merry. I have to find out what was happening in Olivia's life in the weeks before she was killed. You know that, right?"

"Yes."

"So, if there's anything else you can tell me—"

"There isn't."

"You spoke to her on the phone last night, right?"

"Yes."

"Tell me about the conversation."

"I asked if we were still on for today. She said we were. That was it."

"No hint that she was upset? Nothing that would make you think she was in danger?"

"I already told Keira there was nothing unusual about the conversation. Not that one. Not the one before it. Not any of the conversations Olivia and I had. Our discussions were always about kids and jobs and what we were going to make for dinner. Mundane things that really didn't matter much."

"Did she seem happy here?"

"Usually. She loved her job and the twins. Sometimes, though, she seemed a little down. Like maybe she was missing home."

"It's not surprising that she'd be homesick sometimes."

"I guess not, but she left Ireland after her mother died because she wanted a fresh start. Now everything she wanted, all her dreams, they've died with her." Merry blinked rapidly, her eyes filling with tears, and he patted her hand, warmth seeping through him at the contact.

Face-to-face, looking straight into Merry's deep brown eyes, he knew two things for sure. First, he was as attracted to her now as he'd been the first moment he'd seen her. Second, she hadn't told him everything she knew.

It was his job to find out what she was hiding, to figure out if it connected to Olivia's murder. His job. His duty. All part of the same thing, and he wouldn't let Merry stand in the way of that. No matter how attractive and compelling he found her.

He placed his coffee cup in the deep porcelain sink. "I think that'll do it for today. I'll stop by again tomorrow."

"Tomorrow?" She sounded appalled, her dark eyes wide, her freckles stark against smooth, pale skin.

"Will that be a problem?"

"No. I just…I've told you everything I can. What good will another meeting do?"

"Telling me everything you can is a lot different than telling me everything you know."

"I don't know what you're talking about," she said, but the shadows in her eyes said something different.

"You know, Merry—" he stepped close, cupped her jaw, her skin silky smooth beneath his hand "—you've lived in Fitzgerald Bay for a year. We've been out together, spent a couple of hours talking to each other, but I still don't know much about you."

She stiffened, her jaw tightening beneath his palm. "Since we're not dating, you know enough."

"That's what I thought, too. Until you started lying to me." He stepped back, watching as his meaning settled in and over her.

"I—"

"I have a lot of work to do. I'll be back tomorrow."

Sometime between now and then, you might want to decide whether continuing your lies is worth losing everything."

"What are you talking about?"

"Withholding information and evidence from the police is a crime you could go to jail for, Merry."

"You can't be serious!" Something flashed in her eyes, a terror so deep that Douglas almost regretted the threat.

Almost.

But he had a job to do, a murderer to find. Olivia deserved justice. He planned to get it for her, and he planned to do it quickly.

He couldn't allow the investigation to go on too long without a suspect. If he did, people might do exactly what he feared and point their fingers at Charles.

The Fitzgerald family motto had been stamped onto his heart before he was old enough to know what it meant. He lived it, breathed it, believed it.

God first.

Family second.

Duty to the community after that.

Olivia's murder touched on all those things, and he'd push for answers until he found the person who killed her.

Push no matter how uncomfortable pushing might be.

Push no matter the terror he saw in Merry's eyes.

Push, because he had a feeling she was the key to solving the case.

If she was, there was nothing she could do, nothing she could say that could make him go away.

FOUR

He meant it.

The coldness in Douglas's eyes left no doubt about his intentions. He'd be back tomorrow, and he'd ask more questions. If he didn't get what he wanted, he'd come back again and again and again.

Merry didn't need time to decide if continuing to lie was worth going to jail over. She couldn't go to jail. Couldn't leave Tyler. Couldn't bear to imagine what would happen to him if anyone found out....

But no one would.

Douglas was interested only in the murder investigation, not Merry's past. As long as she was up front about her friendship with Olivia, she had nothing to worry about.

Only she'd made a promise and breaking it seemed paramount to dishonoring Olivia's memory.

Please, God, help me know what to do.

Break the promise? Keep it?

She took a deep breath as she followed Douglas to the door, tried to look into his eyes and convince him that she had nothing to hide. "I haven't lied to you."

"But you haven't told me the whole truth, either. That's a problem for me, Merry. I want full disclosure. I want everything that you know about Olivia. Everything she said,

everything you thought she might have meant. *Everything.*"
He hooked a strand of hair behind her ear, his fingers lingering on the tender flesh there. She felt his warmth seeping through her, felt herself giving into his urgency and her own need to tell him what he wanted to know.

I trust you more than I trust anyone else in Fitzgerald Bay, Merry, and I'm trusting you with this. Promise me you'll keep it secret. Don't tell another soul about it, Keep it locked away until my sweetheart comes for it. Promise me.

Olivia's words seemed to drift in on the frigid winter air as Douglas opened the door. They sealed Merry's lips, insisted that the promise be kept, the secret hidden.

"Think about it, okay?" he said softly, and Merry nodded, afraid that if she spoke, she might say what she shouldn't, reveal what she'd promised not to.

"Mommy, is he leaving?" Tyler appeared at the top of the stairs, his chubby cheeks flushed with excitement, his black eyes flashing with curiosity.

"Yes."

"But I didn't show him my other police car." He held up a small police car, his sleeve riding up just enough to show the bottom edge of the scar. A purplish smudge against tan skin. Barely noticeable, but Merry noticed, and she wanted to race up the stairs, pull his sleeve down.

"I haven't given you permission to come out of your room, Ty. Go back in there."

"But he's leaving!"

"For now. I'll be back tomorrow, sport," Douglas responded, and Merry was sure she heard a threat in his words.

"See my other car?" Tyler held out the car again, the sleeve riding up even farther, revealing more of the scar. Merry's heart skipped a beat, then raced on, the sloshing pulse of it stealing her breath. If Douglas noticed the purplish mark, if he asked about it…

"Go to your room, Tyler William. This instant." The sharp edge in her tone surprised Tyler as much as it surprised Merry, and he shot her a hurt look before trudging back to his room.

Great.

Could the day get any worse?

"He's got a lot of energy," Douglas said, and Merry braced herself for the questions she knew would come.

Because, of course, the day *could* get worse.

"That's for sure."

"He doesn't look much like you."

"He looks like his father." It's what she always said, and she assumed it was true.

"You were married?"

"No."

"I see," he said, and she was pretty sure he did see. All her half truths and evasions. Her way of living for four long years.

"If you don't need anything else—"

"Do you share custody with Tyler's father?" He cut her off, and she knew he'd go when he was ready. Not a minute sooner.

"He's not in our life." *Stick to the truth. Keep it simple. Don't offer more than what is asked for.* Those were the rules she lived by, and she followed them as if her life depended on it.

Her life probably *did* depend on it.

"Has he ever been?"

Keep it simple.

"No."

"Is there a reason for that?"

"Not one I want to share."

"All right." Douglas studied her intently, his eyes dusky blue, his expression unreadable, and she wondered what he *did* see.

More than she wanted him to.

Wasn't that the reason why she'd told him things weren't working out between them?

She had too many secrets, and he'd asked too many questions and lying to someone she respected and admired and wanted to get to know wasn't something she'd been willing to do.

She still wasn't willing to do it, but she couldn't tell him the truth without losing everything she cared about most.

"I guess I'll see you tomorrow," she said, lamely filling the silence.

"See you then," he responded as he walked down the porch steps, zipping his bomber jacket against the cold.

He moved with an effortless confidence. Why wouldn't he? He was a Fitzgerald in Fitzgerald Bay. Surrounded by family and love. Embraced by a community that knew and loved him.

Merry's siblings were in Boston, and she couldn't return there. Her mother and father had been gone for a decade.

All she had was her son and way too many secrets.

Sometimes, that made life a little lonelier than she wanted it to be.

Douglas tipped his hat as he got into his SUV, flashing the charming smile that had given him a reputation as the most eligible bachelor in town. Merry had heard plenty about his single status during her first months in Fitzgerald Bay. As a matter of fact, more than one of the older ladies in her Bible study had suggested that Douglas would be perfect husband *and* father material. Maybe that's why she'd given into temptation and gone out with him. Or maybe she'd just been desperate to connect, to feel normal and unencumbered. To be young and carefree and filled with dreams.

Whatever the case, she'd made a mistake. She couldn't afford to make another one. She closed the door, turning the bolt and setting the alarm, checking the windows and back door. Going through the ritual that had been part of her life for four years.

When she finished, she went into Tyler's room, put her hand on his solid little shoulder. "I'm sorry I snapped at you, sweetie, but you need to obey me the first time. Not the second or third."

"I'm sorry, too, Mommy. Next time I'll listen better." He wrapped his arms around her waist, buried his face in her side. Precocious and busy, he had a sweet nature that made him very easy to love.

"Good. Now, give me a kiss, and then we'll go down and have some dinner."

"Kiss!" He pressed a kiss to her cheek, giggling as she tickled his belly.

"Let's go." She took his hand, and he bounced out of the room. Bounced down the steps. Bounced into the kitchen. Preschool teachers were already talking about attention deficit and hyperactivity. Very bright. Extremely likable. Too busy. Too active. Too talkative. The labels had been stamped on his forehead, and Merry knew they'd follow him into kindergarten in the fall. She'd been hoping that being in a small community, having friends and teachers who accepted him as he was would smooth the transition into school. That was one of the reasons she'd stayed in Fitzgerald Bay longer than she'd stayed anywhere since she'd left Boston.

"Is the policeman really gone?" Tyler asked, and Merry nodded.

"Yes."

"But he's coming back tomorrow?"

"That's right. Only tomorrow, you're not going to open the door for him. You're going to let me do that."

"But—"

"Tyler, it's one of our rules that can't be broken, remember? You are never to open the door unless I give you permission." Because the thought of him opening the door for a stranger with his black eyes and deeply tanned complexion filled Merry with terror.

"I remember. I won't open the door again. I promise." He threw his arms around her waist, his chubby cheek pressed to her thigh.

"When you make a promise you have to keep it. Right?" *Even if the promise costs you everything.*

"Yes. Can I have a cookie?"

"After dinner." Which couldn't come soon enough. She needed time to think. Not easy to come by with Tyler awake and active. She wouldn't have it any other way, though.

"When is dinner?"

"Soon."

"Chicken nuggets?"

"Fish."

"Yuck." Tyler frowned, and Merry did her best not to smile.

"Be happy we have food."

"I'd be happier if the food was chicken." He ran to the living room window, pressed his face against the glass. "Is he really coming back?"

"Yes, Tyler. Tomorrow."

Unless she could think of a way to get out of it. A way that wouldn't make Douglas more suspicious than he already was.

Or, maybe she didn't have to think of a way. Maybe, she just needed to *make* a way. Pack a bag for herself and Tyler, take the bus south or west or even north, ride until she reached a place where she and Ty could easily get lost in the teeming mill of humanity. She'd done it before, been successful before. She could do it again. Only, she had a feeling that Douglas would track her down. He might be charming and easy to look at, but he wouldn't be easy to cross.

The phone rang, and she answered quickly, eager for a distraction. "Hello?"

"Merry? It's Fiona." Her boss Fiona Fitzgerald's voice poured across the line, and Merry blinked back the tears she'd been fighting all afternoon. Melting into a blubbering puddle of sorrow and fear wouldn't do her any good, and it would only scare Tyler.

"I guess you've heard the news, Fiona."

"I don't think there's anyone in town who hasn't. How are you holding up?"

"I'm okay."

"Are you sure? *I'm* shaken, and I wasn't the one who found Olivia."

"I'm sure." An image of the body lying below the cliff, arms and legs splayed, blond hair dark from salty spray flashed through her mind, and she shoved it away. She wanted to remember Olivia vibrantly alive. Not broken and still.

"Douglas said he's going to stop by your place tomorrow. Would you like me to come by, too? I can bring Sean. He and Tyler can play together."

"I can't ask you to do that, Fiona."

"You're not asking. I'm offering." A widow with a six-year-old son, Fiona had proven to be an understanding employer. She allowed Merry time off when she needed it, understood the demands of single motherhood.

"And I appreciate it, but I don't want you and Sean to give up your afternoon for us. Why don't you bring him over when the Reading Nook closes next week? We can have dinner together." *If* Merry was still around, and the way that things were looking, she wasn't sure she would be.

But she didn't want to leave.

She liked Fitzgerald Bay. She liked the people she'd met there. She liked her little house and her landlady. But more than all of that, she liked the home she was making for Tyler. A place to settle, that's what she'd seen when she'd driven into the little fishing town. She didn't want to have to run from it.

"Are you sure, Merry? My brother is charming, but he can be pushy. I don't mind being a buffer."

"Am I going to need a buffer?"

"That depends on how much Douglas thinks you know."

"I've already told him what I know, so I'm sure I'll be fine." She hoped, because from the sound of things, Douglas might have mentioned his suspicions to Fiona. Or, at least, asked enough questions about Merry that Fiona sensed his suspicions. Either way, things weren't looking good.

Get out of town, Merry.

Go. Before he finds you.

Promise me.

The words whispered out of the past, the desperation in them reaching across four years, filling Merry with the same fear she'd felt the day Nicole had said them.

"If you change your mind, let me know. And if you

need some time off work—" Fiona broke into her thoughts, and Merry forced herself to focus on the conversation.

"I won't." Sitting around the house, reliving the moment that she'd looked down and seen Olivia's body was the last thing she wanted to do.

"I'll see you at church tomorrow."

"See you then." If she didn't pack everything and leave town.

She hung up and walked into the living room, looked out onto the quiet street. Darkness swept in from the east, casting shadowy dusk across the yard. Flakes of snow fell, swirling onto golden grass and black pavement. A beautiful evening, and Olivia wasn't around to enjoy it.

Merry wiped away hot tears.

"Are you sad, Mommy?" Tyler tugged her hand, and she looked down into his face.

"I'm hungry. Want to help me make the fish?" She sidestepped his question, pulling him toward the refrigerator.

She'd think about Olivia after Tyler went to bed.

She'd think about the promise she'd made to her.

Think about the secret she'd hidden beneath the floorboard in her closet.

Think about truth and lies and the fine line between protecting someone and obstructing justice.

Think.

Pray.

Hope that God would help her figure out what to do, because she didn't know, couldn't decide.

Right path.

Wrong path.

She'd stopped knowing which one she was on years ago.

Now she all wanted was to keep Tyler safe.

Please, God, help me keep him safe.

FIVE

Midnight came and went. Two o'clock. Three. Sleepless, Merry listened to the house groan and the wind howl. Lonely. That's how she felt. Lonely and unsure.

All the prayer and thinking hadn't changed anything. She still didn't know what to do.

"Mommy?" Tyler called out above the sound of the howling wind, and she hurried across the hall and into his room.

"What is it, sweetie? Did the wind wake you?" She flicked on the light, her heart jumping as she saw the empty bed.

"The policeman is back." Tyler stood near the window that overlooked the front yard, his black hair mussed, his blue pajamas twisted around his hips.

"It's too early for him to be here." She walked to the window and lifted Tyler. Wide awake, he was wiggly and active and very difficult to hug. Sleepy, he cuddled close, his arms wrapping around her neck.

"He is there, Mommy. See?" He pointed out the window, and she looked, her heart skipping a beat as she spotted a dark SUV parked at the curb. Tinted windows blocked her view of the interior.

She stepped back, pulled Tyler a little closer.

"That's not a police car, Ty. It's someone else's."

"But I saw him. He was coming right up to the front door."

His words shivered along her spine and filled her with cold, hard dread. No one wandered around the neighborhood at three in the morning unless they were up to no good.

She flicked off the light, set Tyler on his bed. "Go back to sleep, sweetie. We've got church in a few hours, and you don't want to be a grumpy bear."

"But he's coming, Mommy. I want to show him my other cars."

"Go to sleep." She dropped a kiss on his head and walked back to the window, her heart beating a hard, heavy rhythm.

Outside, darkness shadowed the yard, but she was sure she saw footprints in the blanket of white snow.

Go down. Look out the living room window and the peephole in the door.

She knew what she had to do.

Knew it, but didn't want to.

She'd never been overly brave. Mice freaked her out. Surprises made her unhappy. But she was a mother. A single mother. No hero husband was going to run to the rescue and take care of things, and she couldn't wait around and hope that Tyler had been mistaken. If someone was wandering around outside the house, she needed to know it, and the only way to know was to look.

Go. Now!

She kept the lights off as she walked down the stairs, her hand sliding along the glossy wood banister, her pulse thrumming with fear. A quick peek through the peephole revealed nothing, and she moved to the living room window, the hair on the back of her neck standing on end, every nerve alive as she peered into the yard.

The wind swept powdery snow across the road and bowed the pine tree that stood at the corner of the front yard. Long shadows danced beneath the streetlights. Human? Inorganic? The white picket fence that she'd painted in the summer seemed to bend beneath the strength of the wind, and the gate swung eerily. Had Douglas latched it when he left? Had someone else unlatched it?

Something moved, and she jumped, biting back a scream as one of Tyler's toys rolled in the wind.

There! Just a few feet from the porch. Footsteps in the snow.

Someone *had* been there.

Someone might *still* be there.

Ice flowed through her blood, her pulse racing with terror. She grabbed the phone, dialing 9-1-1 as a shadow separated itself from behind the pine tree. Tall. Thin. She couldn't make out features or clothes, couldn't see more than shadows and shapes.

"9-1-1. What is the state of your emergency?"

"I need the police. Someone is outside my house," she whispered, though she knew whoever was outside couldn't hear. Whispered because fear trapped the words in her throat, made it nearly impossible for her to get them out.

"Is he trying to enter your house?"

"I don't know."

"We'll send a patrol car out. Stay inside until it arrives."

"Okay." She didn't have to be told twice. There was no way she planned to walk outside and investigate. As a matter of fact, she'd rather not investigate from inside.

She stepped away from the window, but kept her eyes on the figure that stood staring at her house. He looked up, seemed to be eyeing something on the second floor. Had Tyler turned on the light? Was he standing in the window of his room?

Her stomach lurched, terror for her son making her shake.

She ran to the front door, flicked the switch to turn on the porch light, hoping to distract the man, maybe even scare him off.

Who was he?

What did he want?

Why was he still standing at the edge of her gated yard?

Questions filled her mind, but she had no answers.

An entire year of peace. An entire year feeling that Fitzgerald Bay might just be the safe haven she'd been searching for.

An entire year, and she'd loved every minute of it.

But it was over.

She felt the truth of that as she moved back to the living room window. The intruder shifted, and she knew he sensed her there in the darkness. She felt the weight of his stare, knew that the world she'd created, the *lie* she'd created was about to unravel.

Please, God, help me keep Tyler safe.

Please, let me keep him.

The interior light of the SUV flashed across blond hair and hollow cheeks as the man jumped into the vehicle.

Blond hair.

Not black.

She should have been relieved, but she wasn't.

Should have relaxed as the SUV drove away, but she couldn't.

Someone had stalked her house while she slept. Someone had stared up at Tyler's room.

Leave town. Don't ever come back.

Nicole's words whispered through her mind. A reminder. A warning. She needed to heed it, needed to pack and go like she had so many times before.

Only things were different this time.

Olivia was dead.

Merry had found the body.

Douglas Fitzgerald was on the hunt for a killer, and he seemed to think Merry knew something that would lead him to his prey.

He'd hunt *her* if she left. That, more than anything, kept her tied to Fitzgerald Bay.

A marked SUV pulled up in front of the house, lights flashing, sirens off. Merry hurried to open the door, stepping onto the porch, cold wind blowing through her flannel pajamas and whipping her hair as a broad figure jogged toward the house. Nearly blind from the wind, snow and hair blowing in her face, she still knew who was coming toward her. She felt it from the tip of her frozen toes to the icy edges of her wild hair.

Felt *him*.

Her stomach clenched.

Not in fear this time.

In acknowledgment.

"I hear you had an early morning visitor." Douglas's voice flowed over her, deep and rich as dark chocolate and even more comforting. She wanted to throw herself into his arms, bury her face against his chest and confess everything. Every secret, every fear.

Stupid.

Foolhardy.

She stepped back into the house, her heart thundering with the need to confess it all, with the desire to share her burden with someone else.

But the consequences would be too great, the risks far outweighing any benefit.

"Yes. He was in the yard, staring at the house."

"Did he try to get in?" He repeated the question the 9-1-1 operator had asked, flecks of snow melting in his black hair as he urged her farther into the house and closed the door.

"I don't think so."

"Tell me what you saw." He pulled out a small notepad, wrote quickly as she described the SUV, the tall, lean man, the feeling that he was staring right at her.

"Did you recognize him? Was he someone you've seen before?" Douglas looked up from his notes, his eyes searching into hers. Concern. Compassion. Strength. She saw them all in the depth of his gaze.

Saw them. Wanted to cling to them.

She swallowed down the desperate need to tell him what she feared—that Tyler's father had come looking for his son.

Come looking for revenge.

"No." Her voice shook, her hand trembling as she brushed cold, wet curls from her cheek.

"Here. Come sit down while I take a look around outside." He led her to the love seat in the living room, urging her onto the cushions, his hands gentle and warm through her flannel sleeves.

Flannel sleeves?

She glanced down at her faded blue pajamas. Pink and yellow hearts danced in wavy lines across fabric that had seen better days, and she blushed, yanking the knit throw from the back of the love seat and pulling it around her shoulders.

As if that would help.

He'd already seen everything there was to see.

Wild, wet hair.

Faded pajamas.

Multicolored toenails peeking out from too-long cuffs.

As if he sensed her thoughts, his gaze dropped to her feet, to the toenails she'd let Tyler paint green and orange and purple.

"Nice." His lips quirked, and she blushed again.

"I thought you were going to check on things outside."

"I am." *In my own good time.*

She was sure she heard the words, though he didn't speak them. Didn't do anything but smile and turn away. Walk out the front door.

She stood, dragging the blanket more tightly around her shoulders, watching from the window as he criss-crossed the front yard, stopped near the pine tree, bent down, studying something.

Having him there felt better than it should.

Safer than it should.

He looked up, and she could see his eyes gleaming in the darkness, knew he was watching her watch him. Her heart jumped, her pulse raced.

Fool!

The last person who should be making her heart jump and her pulse race was Douglas Fitzgerald. *Captain* Douglas Fitzgerald.

She turned away, walking into the kitchen and flipping on the light. She needed caffeine to clear her head. Maybe one of the double chocolate cookies she'd baked earlier to settle her churning stomach.

She *needed* to pull herself together.

Someone had been outside her house, but that didn't mean her world was crumbling. It didn't mean Tyler's father had found them. It didn't mean Merry needed to throw herself into strong capable arms and beg for help.

But maybe she wanted to.

Maybe, for once, she didn't want to go it alone.

She shivered, wiping away water that dripped from her hair and down her cheek, wishing she hadn't promised to keep Olivia's secret. If she hadn't, she could have given Douglas what Olivia had left with her. One less secret to keep. One less burden to bear.

Someone rapped on the back door, and Merry jumped.

"Merry? Open up," Douglas called out, and she hurried to unlock the door.

"Thanks. It's wicked out there tonight." He brushed snow from his coat, brushed it from soft black hair.

"Want some coffee?" She turned away, afraid if she didn't, she'd look into his eyes and just keep on looking.

"Sure." He accepted the steaming mug, wrapped broad hands around the sturdy porcelain. "You have an alarm system, don't you?"

"I had one installed when I moved in. Ida said it wasn't necessary, but I feel more secure if I have one. Not that I don't think Fitzgerald Bay is safe, I do, but you just never know. I mean, look what..." *Stop talking. Stop right now!*

She took a deep breath, tried to quiet her nerves and still her tongue.

"Look what happened to Olivia?"

"Yes."

"It's good you're thinking that way. The person who was outside your house wasn't just in your front yard. He walked from his car to your porch, then around to the back door. He stopped at every window on the way there. He wanted a way in. He just didn't find it." He eyed her over the rim of the cup, his eyes blazing.

"What now?" she asked, because she wasn't sure what else to say. She didn't believe the attempt was random. Didn't think someone had chosen her quaint little Cape

Cod over the larger more elaborate homes on the street as the one that would yield good returns on a robbery.

"I'm going to dust for prints. Maybe we'll pull one that matches someone who's already in the system."

"If you do get a match, what then?"

"We'll find our perp."

"You make it sound easy."

"It would be easier if you'd tell me everything you know. Whatever you're hiding, Merry, why don't you tell me about it? Let me help you?" His hands cupped her shoulders, his touch light, but she felt it deeply, felt the connection he was trying to build. That she wanted to build, too.

"I don't need help."

But she did. She'd needed it for a long time. She just hadn't known how to ask, *who* to ask.

Not him.

Not a police officer.

You'll lose everything.

You'll lose Tyler.

"Yeah. You do." His words were as gentle as his touch, and she knew she had to give him something so that he'd go away, leave her to take care of her problems the way she always had. If he didn't, she just might give in to temptation, reveal the darkest, deepest secret she'd ever kept.

"Olivia gave me something when she was visiting." The words tasted like betrayal, and she blinked back tears, Olivia's pretty face and bright blue eyes floating through her mind.

"What?" His tone remained gentle, but she sensed the change in him, the surge of excitement.

"A letter. It's sealed in an envelope. I didn't open it."

"Who is it for?"

"Her sweetheart. She said he might come for her one

day, and she wanted him to know how much she'd cared, how deeply she missed him. She made me promise to keep the letter until her sweetheart came. She just kept saying it over and over again, 'Promise me, Merry. Promise me you won't give it to anyone else but my sweetheart.'" And, now, she was breaking the promise she'd made. A tear trickled down her cheek, but wiping it away would take more energy than she had, and she collapsed into a chair instead, let more tears flow, because she really didn't care about stopping them.

Olivia was dead.

Merry had broken her promise.

"Don't cry." Douglas crouched near the chair, his hand resting on her knee, his blue, blue eyes looking into hers.

"Why shouldn't I? Her sweetheart will never find Olivia now. They'll never have a second chance to make things work." But she did need to stop, because crying made her vulnerable, and she couldn't afford to be that.

Not when she still had so many secrets to keep.

"You did the right thing. That's what you need to re-member and hold on to. Olivia wouldn't have expected anything less from you."

"If it was the right thing, why does it feel so wrong?"

"Because, you're a good person and a loyal friend. So no more tears, okay?" He brushed at the moisture on her cheeks and smiled, but she couldn't smile back.

She stood, let the blanket fall onto the chair. "I'll get the letter for you."

And, then she ran from the room, ran up the stairs and into her cozy bedroom with its antique furniture and tiny closet.

A good person?

He might not think so if he knew the truth.

He's in danger. You have to believe me. Please, leave

town and take him with you. It's the only way to keep him safe.

The words of a desperate teen, the plea of a mother who had probably known she wouldn't live long enough to see her son grown, and Merry had agreed, because she'd wanted to help.

Did that make her a good person or a bad one?

After four years, she still didn't know.

She blinked back more tears as she opened her closet door and pulled up the loose floorboard. Beneath it, a white envelope lay atop a small leather journal. Beside them both, a blue bankbook was rubber banded with a stack of hundred dollar bills.

Too many secrets.

Sometimes, she got really tired of keeping them.

Sometimes, she wished she had one person she could share the burden with. One person she could trust enough to reveal the truth to.

But she didn't.

Not her siblings.

Not her friends.

Certainly not the man who waited for her to return to the kitchen.

She'd do well to keep that in mind.

"Merry? Are you okay?" Douglas called from the bottom of the stairs, and her heart jumped in fear and in anticipation.

She acknowledged them both as she grabbed the envelope and let the floorboard fall back into place, hiding her secrets once again.

SIX

A letter from Olivia to her sweetheart.

That's what Merry had been hiding?

He wasn't sure he was convinced.

It's what she wanted Douglas to believe she'd been hiding.

He tapped his fingers against satiny wood, waiting expectantly as Merry started down the steps, a white envelope clutched in her hand.

"Here it is." She held out the business-size envelope, her hand steady, her gaze direct. Obviously, she *really* wanted him to believe the letter was it.

But fear still lurked in the depth of her eyes. He could see it, feel it as he took the letter from her hand.

"Are you going to open it?" she asked and he nodded. He had no choice. Private or not, the letter had to be opened.

"Can I have it back after you're finished with it?"

"It's evidence. We won't be able to release it until the case is closed." He slid his finger under the taped flap and opened the envelope, carefully removing a folded sheet of lined paper.

Handwritten in blue ink, the note was less than a half

page long, the words scrawled across the lines in sweeping manuscript. He read it quickly, silently.

Sweetheart,
Being away from you these past months has been torture. There isn't a day that goes by that I don't think of you and regret the decision I made that separated us. I know that you will come looking for me eventually just as I am now searching for you. I am giving this note to a dear friend to keep until the day that we are reunited. If you receive this before we meet again, please know that I have never stopped loving you. You own my heart as surely as the sun owns the day.
All my love forever.

No signature. No name.
Nothing.
Frustrated, Douglas slid it back into the envelope and tucked it into an evidence bag.

"Did it help?" Merry asked, and he met her dark eyes, shook his head.

"Unfortunately, no."

"I'm sorry. I'd hoped it would." The sincerity in her eyes was unmistakable, but he couldn't shake the feeling that she had more secrets, more things she needed to share.

"You keep saying you want to help, Merry, but I keep getting the impression that you're not telling me everything you know."

"I am."

"That's what you said earlier. Now, I'm standing here with a letter in my hand. A letter you didn't tell me about fourteen hours ago."

"I promised—"

"What else are you hiding?"

"Nothing."

"You're lying." He didn't have time to beat around the bush, didn't have time to wait her out. He needed everything she knew now. Not tomorrow or next week or next month. A killer was on the loose, and there was no telling if that person would strike again.

"I don't know anything else about Olivia. Nothing that would lead me to believe she was in danger. Nothing that might help you find her boyfriend. That's the truth." Something about the way she said it made him take a step closer, look down into her soft, pretty face. Round eyes and high cheekbones, light brows that arched perfectly over thick, golden eyelashes, she looked fresh and sweet and innocent, and he wanted to believe her.

I don't know anything else about Olivia.

What *did* she know about, then?

Someone knocked on the door, the sharp rap cutting through the tense silence. Douglas opened the front door, frowned as he saw his father standing on the porch. Dark circles rimmed Aiden's eyes, and he looked a decade older than he had that morning.

"Aren't you supposed to be off duty, Dad?" Douglas refrained from asking if his father was okay. He'd done that one too many times since Olivia's body had been recovered, and Aiden hadn't appreciated it.

"I could ask you the same."

"I was still at the office when the call came in. I figured it would be as easy for me to respond as anyone else. Who called you?"

"Ryan. He said he couldn't sleep and went down to the station to do some research. Vera told him about the emergency call. He called me."

"I'm surprised he's not here."

"Another call came in after you left. Drunk and disorderly. He's taking care of that. Then, he'll be here." Aiden took off his hat, his gaze on Merry. "You've had quite a day, Merry."

"It's been...rough."

"We'll get things sorted out. Did you dust for prints, yet?" he asked Douglas.

"I'm about to."

"Good. Maybe we'll get a print that will match what we pulled from Olivia's apartment."

"Tonight's perp was male. The two prints we were able to identify from Olivia's place belonged to a woman. Lila Kensington. Did Olivia ever mention her, Merry?" Because Charles didn't seem to know who she was or why she would have been in the apartment. A background check had revealed Lila Kensington's last known address in Boston, Massachusetts. Her last known employer had been the city of Boston public schools. Which was why her prints were in the system. No police record. Nothing to indicate the woman was a murderer.

But her fingerprints were in Olivia's apartment, and Olivia was dead.

"No," Merry responded, her voice raspy and hollow.

"You're sure?"

"Yes." The fear in her eyes, the tense way she held herself gave the lie away.

"Merry—"

She glanced up the stairs, cocked her head to the side. "Tyler is calling me. I'll be back down in a few minutes."

She didn't wait for a response, just turned tail and ran up the stairs.

"Did you hear her son?" Aiden asked, and Douglas shook his head.

"No."

"Me, neither. Why do you think she's so jumpy?"

"I don't know, but I plan to find out."

"Could be she knows more than she's saying about what happened to Olivia."

"She has secrets, for sure. Here's one of them." He handed his father the letter, watched while Aiden read it.

"So, Olivia had a boyfriend."

"A sweetheart."

"We need to find out who that was. I don't suppose Merry knows."

"She says she doesn't."

"I don't." Merry carried Tyler from his room.

Dark head pressed to her shoulder, one fist wrapped around a lock of her hair, he looked sleepy and unhappy.

"We woke your son. I'm sorry about that." Aiden patted Tyler on the back.

"He was already awake, but I'd really like to get him settled and back to sleep." She hinted broadly, her gaze on the front door, the floor, the wall. Everything and anything but Douglas or his father.

"We're going to dust for prints, and then we'll be out of your hair." Aiden walked out the front door, and Douglas could have followed.

Could have.

But there were tear tracks on Merry's cheeks, fear in her eyes. She looked shaken, defeated and terrified, and he wanted to know why.

"You can't keep lying forever. Whatever you're hiding, it's going to come out eventually," he said casually, and the color drained from her face.

"I think I need to sit down." And, she did. No fanfare. No walk to a chair. Just straight down onto a step.

"*I* think—" he crouched down so they were eye to eye "—that you need to tell me what's going on."

"I didn't eat dinner or lunch. Maybe my blood sugar dropped."

"Pretending ignorance isn't going to keep me from pushing for the truth." But she looked awfully pale, her skin completely leached of color, her eyes dark against the pallor. He pressed his palm against the back of her neck, urging her head down toward her knees.

Soft warm skin.

Soft silky hair.

Soft sweet Merry, and all her lies and secrets.

"I'm sorry," she mumbled, and he sighed, his knuckles skimming her cheek as he backed away.

"Me, too. Sorry that you don't trust me enough to tell me why you're so scared."

"It's not about trust."

"Then what *is* it about?"

"Nothing that has to do with your murder investigation." She stood, some of the color returning to her face, her arms still tight around her son.

"The investigation isn't the only thing I'm concerned about, Merry. I'm concerned about you."

"Don't be."

"I'm not sure I have a choice."

"We all have choices."

"Then I guess I'm choosing to be concerned."

"I'd rather you choose something else." She smiled, but it didn't hide the sadness in her eyes.

"You never did tell me why things weren't working out between us."

"I don't think this is a good time to discuss it. I have to get him back to bed." She touched Tyler's hair, walked up the stairs.

She was right.

This wasn't a good time to discuss their relationship.

Or their lack of a relationship.

"Bye, Mr. Policeman." Tyler waved as Merry carried him into his room, the sleeve of his pajamas falling back to reveal a half-dollar-size mark on his wrist. A bruise? No. The mark was raised. Like a ridged scar.

A burn?

That's what it looked like, but Merry disappeared inside Tyler's room too quickly for Douglas to get a better look.

Douglas didn't think she'd be coming out anytime soon. She was done answering questions, but he wasn't done asking them.

Douglas pulled up his hood and stepped into the frigid morning. Deep clouds covered the waning moon and the wind blew snow across his path as he joined his father at the edge of the yard. "See anything that might help?"

"Just what you probably already spotted. Footprints. Size eleven or twelve shoe. Looks like a running shoe. Not a boot. I took a few pictures and I'm trying to cast one of the prints. We'll see if it takes in this weather. If it doesn't, the prints will be gone before the weather clears." Aiden sounded more like himself than he had all day. Confident, self-assured. That was what Douglas expected his father to be. It's what he'd grown up seeing.

"How about prints?"

"Haven't dusted yet. I thought I'd leave that to you."

"Do you think this is connected to Olivia's murder?" Douglas asked as he pulled an evidence kit from his SUV.

"What do you think?"

"It's a stretch to believe it isn't."

"Yet the fingerprints we were able to match from the apartment belonged to a woman and Merry saw a man standing outside her house. So, maybe we *are* dealing with two unrelated crimes." Aiden rubbed the back of his neck, obviously tired and frustrated.

"There were other prints at the apartment we weren't able to match, Dad. There's every possibility that the prints we pull tonight will match up with one of them."

"I'm not sure if that will make things better or worse. Connected crimes or random, we still have a murderer to find. Did you put in a call to Boston P.D.? Maybe they have some information about Lila Kensington that will give us something to work with."

"She's not on their radar. Aside from the prints that were filed when she applied to teach, there's no trace of her in the system." Douglas dusted the first windowsill, picked up a set of smudged prints and moved to the next window.

"Call Boston again in the morning. We need more information, and we need it quickly. A murder in Fitzgerald Bay is big news, and people are talking. They're already speculating about the identity of the killer, offering a hundred different explanations as to why she was murdered." Aiden paused and inhaled deeply. "Your brother's name has already come up."

"That doesn't surprise me. There's been talk around town for a few weeks about Charles and Olivia being in a relationship."

"What! Charles had no interest in Olivia as anything other than a nanny to his children."

"You're preaching to the choir, Dad." And getting more worked up than Douglas had expected.

"I know. It just burns me up the way people around town talk about things that have no basis in fact."

"That's the point, right? They speculated about a relationship that didn't exist, and now they're making up motives for murder out of those unfounded speculations. It's not surprising, and it doesn't mean anything." But Douglas still wanted to name a suspect, give the people in town someone else to talk about.

"Doesn't mean anything? Your brother is a war veteran, a hero who came back to serve his community. He deserves better than whispered accusations." Aiden's voice shook with the depth of his emotion, and Douglas put a hand on his shoulder.

"The people who are whispering are a very small minority, Dad. You know that."

"It still isn't right." Aiden inhaled deeply, shook his head. "We need to find a suspect quickly, because there are people in town who believe we own the police department, and who'll be more than happy to accuse us of tampering with evidence if they think we're trying to protect Charles."

"We're not, so I really don't care what they think."

"You'd better care. If people think we're covering anything up—"

"Why would they? We've always been aboveboard, and we've always conducted ourselves with integrity and honor. The town knows that." Douglas pulled two prints off the back door, wishing he felt as confident as he sounded.

But the Fitzgeralds had represented a large percentage of the police department for as long as there'd been one in town. Because of that, there were people who muttered about nepotism and favoritism. It had never been much of an issue. But then, no Fitzgerald had ever been a target of a murder investigation before.

And no one was now.

Douglas would happily tell that to anyone who cared to mumble and speculate, and he'd happily stand by his words.

His brother hadn't committed a crime, and Douglas would do whatever it took to prove it.

Even make sweet, soft Merry O'Leary cry again.

SEVEN

"Is he here yet?" Tyler jumped from the couch to the love seat, his dark hair falling into his eyes. He needed a haircut. He also needed to stop jumping on the furniture.

Rules were rules.

Even when Merry felt too tired to enforce them.

"Jump on the floor, Ty, not on the furniture."

"Okay, Mommy. Jump, jump, jump, jump, jump." He hopped across the floor, his voice rising louder with every jump. Unlike Merry, the more tired Tyler got, the busier he became. He'd crash eventually, but not before Merry's head exploded. She pressed her fingers to the bridge of her nose and bit back irritation.

"On second thought, how about you find something quiet to do?"

"Play-Doh?"

"Sure. At the table in the kitchen, though. Not out here."

"Jump, jump, jump." Tyler hopped into the kitchen, and Merry pulled out Play-Doh and cookie cutters. That should keep him busy for at least ten minutes.

She glanced at the clock—1:50 p.m. and no sign of Douglas. She'd love to believe he'd forgotten or that he'd decided he didn't need to question her again, but she knew better. Douglas wasn't the kind of guy who forgot things.

He wasn't the kind of guy who missed things. He wasn't the kind of guy who let things go.

She needed to leave. That's what she needed to do.

Needed to run as fast and as far as she could.

Lila Kensington.

The name echoed through her head as she swallowed a couple aspirin and paced back into the living room.

Lila.

Kensington.

Lila.

Kensington.

Douglas had asked if Olivia had ever mentioned the name, and Merry had told the truth. Olivia had never mentioned the name. No one had. Not in four years.

Now someone had. Not just someone. Douglas. He wouldn't stop asking questions until he knew who Lila was. Merry knew that and knowing it terrified her.

It wouldn't take long for Douglas to find people connected to Lila, and once he found them, he'd only have to ask for a picture.

Four years.

It seemed like a lifetime.

In some ways, it was.

But people in Boston would remember. Her friends, her coworkers, her siblings. Douglas would ask, they'd pull out photos, and then he'd realize that Lila Kensington and Merry O'Leary were the same person.

She shuddered, terrified of what that would mean for her and for Tyler.

Everything she'd worked so hard for was falling apart, and she didn't know how to keep doing what she'd been doing since Nicole had placed Tyler into her arms, didn't know how to keep up the charade.

Didn't know how she could stop without losing her son.

She walked to the window, stared out into bright sunlight. Crisp white snow shimmered in the sun, whatever footprints had been in the yard hidden by a fresh layer of powder. Hidden or not, Merry knew they were there. Someone had been creeping around the house, trying to find a way in.

Who?

Why?

The questions had kept her awake long after Tyler finally drifted to sleep.

The questions.

The fear.

The name.

Her entire world coming undone.

Leave town. Don't come back.

Nicole's words seemed to fill the room, fill Merry's heart, and she wanted to do exactly what she'd done all those years ago.

Run.

Douglas's SUV pulled into the driveway, and her stomach lurched.

She couldn't run.

Not unless she wanted to be pursued by a man who would never ever give up the chase.

She opened the door before he knocked, stepping aside as he and Keira walked into house.

Two officers?

Merry wasn't sure what that meant, but she doubted it meant anything good.

"Sorry about the wait, Merry. We've been a little busy at the station." Douglas offered a quick easy smile, his striking blue eyes just warm enough to make her wonder if things would go better than she'd imagined.

"It's no problem. Ty and I were just hanging around the house."

"You know my sister? Officer Keira Fitzgerald."

"Yes. We've seen each other at the Reading Nook and at church, and we spoke yesterday. Come in and sit down. I was going to start a fire, but I'm out of wood. I need to buy some, but time keeps getting away from me." There she went, offering information that no one had asked for. A bad habit she didn't seem to be able to break, and one that was bound to get her into trouble if she wasn't careful.

"Actually, Merry—" Douglas grabbed her arm, pulling her to a stop "—I think that we'd be better off conducting the interview down at the station."

"At the station?" She parroted his words, fear such a hard, sharp knot in her stomach she thought she might be sick. Did he know? Had he already discovered the truth? "Am I being arrested?"

"Of course you're not," Keira responded, but her reassurance did nothing to ease Merry's fear.

"Keira will stay here with Tyler. Unless you'd like to bring him along?"

She *didn't* want to bring him along.

She didn't want to bring *herself* along.

"I'm sure I can answer your questions here as easily as I can down at the station."

"We pulled a print from your back door last night. We need to take your prints, see if they're a match. You could come in tomorrow to have it done, but you're probably working. Besides, putting it off will slow the investigation. I'm sure you don't want to do that." Douglas smiled, but there was a hard edge in his voice and in his eyes.

They needed to take her fingerprints, try to match them to the ones they'd already found?

Of course they did.

The headache pounding behind Merry's eyes intensified, and she felt blinded by it and her terror. "I really don't feel well."

"I'm sorry to hear that, but we need to get this done today."

"She really doesn't look all that good, Captain. Maybe an extra day won't hurt." Keira offered Merry a look of sympathy, but the calculation in her eyes was unmistakable.

Was this their version of good cop/bad cop?

Did they already know the truth?

Were they going to take Tyler while she was at the police station?

Her breathing hitched, and she couldn't suck in enough oxygen.

"Hey, calm down. You're not in any trouble. I just need to ask you a few more questions." Douglas pressed a warm palm against her cheek, his voice soothing and gentle, his touch light as he stared into her eyes, willed her to breathe again.

And, suddenly, she could.

Breathe.

Think.

They couldn't know.

Not yet.

Not until they got her prints and, by the time they figured things out, she would be gone. Pursued by Douglas or not, she *had* to go.

Rough calluses rasped against her skin as Douglas's hand slipped from her cheek to her shoulder and rested there. Strong, supportive, undemanding. For a moment, she let herself imagine that he was on her side. That she didn't need to run from him. That running *to* him was the only thing that could save her and Tyler.

A foolish thought.

A foolish dream.

But looking into his steady gaze, she could almost imagine it coming true.

"Better?" he asked, and she nodded, afraid to speak. Afraid the truth would spill out, and that she'd beg him for the help she'd needed for four long years.

Beg him and destroy everything.

"You sure, Merry? Because, you look like you're about to collapse." Keira frowned, and Merry swallowed hard, trying to clear her throat, make room for the words she needed to say.

"I'm fine. I just… It was a long night."

"Today will be shorter. How about we get going? The sooner you get down to the station, the quicker we can be done." Douglas squeezed her shoulder, stepped away, and she wanted to follow him, lean her pounding head against his chest and cry until there wasn't a tear left.

Cry because Olivia was dead.

Cry because Merry's time in Fitzgerald Bay was coming to an end.

Cry because she'd been holding so much in for so long.

She blinked hard, turned toward the kitchen, refusing the tears and the temptation. "That's fine. Let me remind Tyler of the rules, and then we can go."

She thought she'd have a few seconds to pull Tyler's sleeve down, remind him that he didn't need to tell Keira about all the places they'd been, the houses they'd lived in. All the times they'd left town in the middle of the night.

But both Fitzgeralds followed her into the kitchen, and she didn't have time for anything but a quick peck on Tyler's cheek and a reminder that he was to be on his best behavior.

The next thing she knew, Keira was sitting beside Tyler, molding a police car out of Play-Doh and Douglas was ushering her out of the kitchen.

Merry grabbed her coat from the closet, her entire being protesting.

She couldn't lose Tyler.

Couldn't.

"You really don't look good, Merry. Are you sure you're not going to collapse on me?" Douglas asked, his deep blue gaze sweeping from the tip of her black boots to the top of her frizzy-haired head. He didn't offer to let her stay home, though. Of course he didn't.

"I'm okay. I'm just not sure leaving Tyler with Keira is a good idea. Let me call my landlady. I'm sure Ida won't mind—"

"Keira is used to kids, and Tyler seems comfortable with her." He opened the door, pressed a palm to Merry's lower back. She could feel the heat of it through her coat and sweater, feel it burning its way up her spine.

Please, don't make me do this.

She wanted to beg like a child, but that would only lead to more questions.

Wanted to drag her feet but knew it wouldn't do any good.

She was being taken to the police station for fingerprinting.

Nothing she could do but go.

Nothing she could do but cooperate.

For now.

She got into the SUV, buckling her seat belt as Douglas closed the door, sealing her into the still-warm vehicle. It smelled of leather and pine and something indefinable and decidedly masculine.

Douglas.

His warmth. His scent. Wrapping her in a comfortable cocoon that made her want to close her eyes, forget everything for a little while.

"You can save us both some time and effort, Merry, and tell me everything now." His words were like ice water in the face, and she jerked, looked into his eyes.

"I've already told you everything."

"You know who Lila Kensington is."

"No." She lied.

Lied, because she had no choice.

"Right." He shoved the key into the ignition, pulled away from the little Cape Cod that Merry loved so much.

"What's that supposed to mean?" she asked, because she knew he expected a response, and it was all she could think of.

"This may be a small town, and I might be a small-town cop, but I've been doing this job for enough years and I've seen enough things to know when someone is hiding something. You are." He drove slowly, passing old Victorian homes and Cape Cod style houses. A few people peeked out their windows as the SUV passed, and Merry knew they were wondering why she was being brought to the police department.

Because I've been lying since I moved here. Because, I'm not who I said I am.

"Olivia never mentioned Lila Kensington." She tried on the truth, let it hang in the air.

"She entrusted you with a letter that was obviously very important to her, but she didn't mention her boyfriend's name or discuss someone who'd visited her on at least one occasion?"

"She was a private person." And Merry had never asked personal questions, because she'd been afraid she'd be asked some in return. Lies weren't her thing. They never had been. Desperation had forced her hand four years ago, but since then, she'd tried to stick as close to the truth as possible.

As close to the truth she'd *created*.

Which wasn't really the truth at all.

"Did she tell you why she came to the States?"

"Charles would probably know more about that than I do." She tensed as they pulled into the parking lot of the Fitzgerald Bay police department.

"Let's get inside and get your prints. Maybe your memory will return while we're taking them."

Not if she passed out cold from sheer terror before then.

"I—"

"Merry, we're going inside, and we're getting your prints. That's the way it's going to work, and sitting out here debating it won't change anything." He got out of the SUV, and she had no choice but to follow.

Out of the vehicle.

Across the parking lot.

Into the small brick building.

Down a narrow hall.

Step by step by step closer to a place she didn't want to be.

"Relax. I'm not taking you to the gallows." Douglas smiled, his face transformed from hard and tough to warm and approachable.

"Then why does it feel like you are?"

"That's a question you'll have to answer yourself. The way I see it, an innocent person has no reason to fear the police." He opened the door to a small office, gestured her inside.

At least it wasn't an interrogation room like she'd seen on TV. No mirrored wall. No stark lights. Just a wood desk and two leather chairs. A bookshelf sat against one wall, file cabinets on either side of it.

"Go ahead and have seat. I need to get the fingerprint kit."

"No need. I already have it." A short dark-haired woman bustled into the room, her gaze resting on Merry for a moment before she turned to Douglas.

"You're always a step ahead of me, Vera." He took the large envelope she offered him.

"That's why I get paid the big bucks, Captain."

"You know I hate when you call me Captain, so cut it out."

"Just trying to be respectful." She flashed a smile in Merry's direction, her curiosity obvious.

"Douglas?" Owen Fitzgerald appeared in the doorway, his hair mused, his tie hanging loose.

"What's up?"

"Sorry to interrupt, but Charles arrived a few minutes ago. We're following up on the interview we conducted yesterday. I thought you might like to be there."

Say yes. Please, say yes.

As long as Douglas was busy interviewing his brother, he couldn't take Merry's prints.

Which meant, she could go home, pack her bags, leave town before her fingerprints were ever taken.

"I'll be right there."

Yes!

"You don't mind waiting, do you, Merry?"

Wait?

It hadn't even occurred to her.

"Tyler—"

"Is fine. We already decided that, remember?" he said

gently, as he helped her out of her coat, hung it on the back of a chair he pulled out for her. Everything smooth and easy and practiced.

Of course.

He'd dated every woman in Fitzgerald Bay.

Or, so the gossip mill said.

He'd know how to help a woman out of her coat, make her feel like waiting for him was the best thing she could do with her time.

Only Merry wasn't waiting for him. She was waiting to be fingerprinted. Something she most definitely did *not* want to do.

"But—"

"I shouldn't be long." He walked out of the room before she could respond.

She stood, grabbed her coat.

"You're not leaving?" Vera asked, and Merry froze.

"I have a son—"

"Keira is with him, right?"

"Yes."

"So, he's fine. You just sit yourself back down and wait." Vera hovered near the door, a frown creasing her smooth brow.

"I will. I just need to get some fresh air." The lie tasted like sawdust, and Merry nearly choked on it.

"You know what I think?" Vera's frown deepened, her dark eyes flashing.

"What?"

"You're pale as a ghost. Have you eaten today?"

"I—"

"You haven't. I know these kinds of things. We'll have to do something about it. We can't have you passing out on the premises. Bad press, and we already have enough of that."

"Bad press because of the murder?"

"Because Charles Fitzgerald hasn't been arrested yet." She spoke quietly, her gaze darting to the hallway.

"Why would he be?"

"Who is the prime suspect in a woman's murder? The husband, boyfriend, lover."

"Charles wasn't any of those things to Olivia."

"You know that, and I know that, but not everyone wants to believe it. I'm going to find you something to eat. You want coffee, too?"

"I—"

"Maybe hot tea instead. With plenty of sugar. You really are pale, and the press will be on us like white on rice if an ambulance shows up and carts someone away." Vera hurried into the hall.

Leave while you can.

The words shouted through Merry's mind, but she couldn't make herself move, not with Vera's words still ringing in the air.

Charles Fitzgerald the prime suspect in Olivia's murder?

No way.

He had nothing to do with it.

Merry didn't know much about Olivia, but she knew the young woman had respected and admired her employer. There'd been nothing untoward going on. Nothing ugly or wrong in their relationship.

How could Merry leave town without making sure people knew that?

How could she stay without risking everything?

"What do I do, Lord?" she whispered the prayer out loud, but only silence answered.

No spark of inspiration.

No clear direction.

Just minutes passing by in silence as she settled back into the chair and waited for Douglas to return.

EIGHT

Charles needed a better alibi. It was as simple as that.

Douglas raked a hand down his jaw and listened to his brother outline his movements from early in the morning the day before Olivia's murder until early in the morning the following day.

Olivia had been killed between midnight and four.

The coroner was positive of that.

Charles was positive *he'd* been in bed sound asleep during the time in question.

Douglas believed him.

He just hoped the town would.

"Are you sure about the timeline you've given?" Douglas asked the same question he'd been asking since he'd seen Olivia's body.

"I'm sure. I made a house call around six, got home at eight. The twins were already asleep. Olivia went to her apartment. That's the last time I saw her." Charles ran a hand over his hair, the scars on his right arm peeking out from beneath the sleeve of his shirt. War wounds from his time in the marines, they were a reminder of just how close Douglas had come to losing him.

He hadn't lost him to the war.

No way would he lose him to the prison system.

He met Owen's eyes. Knew his younger brother was thinking the same thing.

"You didn't hear a car? Didn't wake up for any reason?"

"I wish I *had* heard something. I would have checked things out, and maybe I could have saved her. But the night wasn't any different than any other. I still can't believe she's dead." Charles rubbed the bridge of his nose, the dark shadows beneath his eyes speaking of a sleepless night.

"We'll find her murderer." Douglas patted Charles's shoulder.

"I have no doubt about that, but that won't bring her back. She was way too young to die, and so brutally…" Charles shook his head, his words echoing the feelings and thoughts of the entire Fitzgerald clan.

"We'll find her murderer," Douglas repeated, because it was all he had to offer.

"Have you been able to reach the next of kin?" Charles asked, and Owen shook his head.

"I left a message for Olivia's cousin to call. Hopefully, she'll get back with me soon. If not, I'll call again before the end of the day."

"How about the coroner? Has he been able to offer anything besides the time of death?"

"I thought we were the ones conducting the interview, Charles," Douglas said, and Charles offered a quick smile.

"Sorry. I'm not good at sitting back and letting other people handle things."

"This time, you're going to have to. I'll check in with you later. Merry O'Leary is waiting to be interviewed and fingerprinted. I don't want to keep her waiting much longer." And, he wasn't sure she *would* wait.

He had a feeling she'd run if she could.

Not just from the police station.

From Fitzgerald Bay.

If he didn't know better, he'd think she'd had something to do with Olivia's death, but she'd been home the night of the murder. He'd talked to her neighbors and her landlady, Ida Sanderson, who lived in the Victorian next door to Merry's place. A neighbor had returned home at one o'clock and seen Merry's station wagon parked in her driveway. Another had left for a hospital shift at three and reported the same. Ida had seen Merry's lights on at midnight. No one on the street had heard the station wagon's loud distinctive engine.

He had to admit, he was relieved. Whatever Merry was hiding, it wasn't her guilt.

He grabbed a file folder from Owen's desk and carried it to his office. Someone had closed the door, and he opened it, half expecting Merry to be gone.

She wasn't.

Head down on the desk, an arm beneath her cheek, she seemed to be sleeping soundly.

"Merry?" He touched her shoulder, and she came up swinging, her eyes blank with fear.

"Hey, calm down. It's just me. Douglas."

Her arm fell to her side, and her cheeks blazed with color. "Sorry. I forgot where I was for a minute."

"Yeah? Where exactly did you think you were?"

"B—" she started to say. Stopped. "I guess I was just having a nightmare."

"Must have been pretty intense."

"I don't remember much about it." She backed away, nearly falling over the chair, and he grabbed her arm, felt tense muscles and warm flesh beneath her long-sleeved T-shirt.

His fingers tightened of their own accord, heat shooting up his arm and straight into his heart.

Merry's blush deepened as she stared into his eyes. She felt it, too. The connection. The attraction. He'd seen it in her eyes when they'd had lunch together. *Still* saw it in her eyes. He was sure of that. He just wasn't sure what either of them wanted to do about it.

He released his hold, forced himself to step back. "Better watch it. If you break your leg, I'll have to take you to the hospital instead of home."

"You're taking me home?"

"Eventually."

"Oh." She looked so disappointed, he almost smiled.

"I still need to get your fingerprints, and I still need to ask you a few questions." He gestured for her to sit, then took the seat across from her.

"I've been here too long. Tyler is probably getting worried."

"*He's* getting worried, or you are?"

"I am. I don't like leaving him with people he doesn't know well."

"He didn't know Ida Sanderson the first time you left him with her."

"I know. It's just…"

"What?"

"Nothing. You said you had more questions for me?"

"Fingerprints first."

It didn't take long. Ten minutes tops. But Merry seemed to grow tenser with every passing second, her fingers taut as he maneuvered them, her face pale.

"Is there some reason why you'd rather not have your fingerprints taken?" Douglas asked casually as he handed her a wet wipe to clean her hands.

"No."

"Is there ever going to be a point when you decide you can trust me with the truth?"

She took one deep breath. Another. Finally, she tossed the wet wipe into the trash can and met his eyes. "I really do need to get home, Douglas."

He wanted to keep pushing, demand an answer, but she was right. She had to get home. And, *he* had to find a killer. "Have you ever seen this?" He pulled a photo from the file folder, slid it across the table.

"It's a dolphin charm," she said, lifting the photo, studying it.

"That's right."

"It doesn't look familiar."

"So, you don't recall Olivia owning a charm bracelet or necklace that might have had a silver dolphin charm on it?"

"No. Why? Was it found…with her?"

"At the scene, but we're going to keep that quiet for a while. Okay?"

"Sure." She looked at the photo for another minute, then slid it back to him. "Olivia had a ring that she inherited from her mother. She wore that a lot, but I'm sure she never wore a charm bracelet. At least not when we were around each other."

Nothing helpful there. Her answer was the same as the one Charles had given. When it came to Olivia Henry it seemed there were more questions than answers. She'd been in town for three months, but no one seemed to know what had brought her to Fitzgerald Bay or why she'd stayed.

Funny, no one seemed to know that about Merry, either.

"What brought *you* to Fitzgerald Bay, Merry?" he asked, expecting her to balk or evade the way she did every time he asked a personal question.

Instead, she shrugged, smiled. "My parents brought me here when I was a kid. I loved it, and I wanted to share the experience with Tyler. We came for a visit, but it's such a wonderful town, I decided to stay."

The answer rolled off her tongue as if she'd rehearsed it a hundred times.

"Just like that, you decided to move?"

"Not really. I was laid off from my previous job as a teacher, and it seemed as good a time as any to start fresh in a new town with a new job."

"So, you're a teacher?"

"*Was* a teacher. Now, I lead story time at your sister's book store." Her smile tightened, but she continued to answer, and Douglas wondered how far he could push before she pushed back.

"Where did you teach?"

"I thought you wanted to ask me questions about Olivia?"

"I did. Now, I want to ask some questions about you."

"And *I* want to go home. Unless you have a reason to keep me here, that's what I'm going to do." She stood, and he knew he'd found the place where his pushing ended and hers began.

Not far.

Not far at all.

He grabbed her hand before she could walk out the door, tugging her to a stop. "You can't run away forever, Merry."

"Who says I'm running?"

"Aren't you?"

"No."

"Then, why not tell me where you're from? Why not explain how you really ended up in Fitzgerald Bay."

"I—"

"You know I can run a background check, right? It won't take long to find out everything there is to know about you. Where you were born, who your parents were, whether or not there's some deep dark reason why you're trying to hide your past."

She paled but didn't respond.

"That's the hard way for both of us. The easy way is for you to tell me everything. All the stuff that you're so determined to keep hidden. Whatever it is, I'll help you deal with it." He eased his grip, his fingers skimming along the tender flesh of her inner wrist as he released her.

She studied his face, her eyes dark and moist with tears. "Maybe—"

"Douglas! We've got trouble." Owen ran into the office, and whatever Merry had planned to say, whatever secrets she might have revealed were lost.

"What kind of trouble?"

"There's been a shooting."

"Where?"

"Merry's place. Keira just called it in."

"Tyler!" Merry shoved passed Owen, ran into the hall.

"Running off half-cocked and getting yourself killed isn't going to help your son." Douglas snagged the back of her shirt, and she whirled around, tears streaming down her cheeks.

"Standing here isn't going to help him, either." She tried to pull away, but he grabbed her shoulders.

"Then, sit. I'll call you as soon as we finish at your place."

"I'm not going to *sit* when my son could be injured. Maybe even—"

"Tyler is fine," Owen said, and Merry turned the full force of her dark brown gaze on him.

"Are you sure?"

"Yes. The shooter fired a couple shots from the street. Took out one of the windows, but no one was hurt."

"Thank God." Her creamy skin had gone parchment pale, her freckles standing out in stark contrast against the pallor.

"You're not going to pass out on me, are you?" Douglas asked, wrapping an arm around her waist.

She managed to shake her head.

"Go back in my office and wait. I'll come for you as soon as we're finished at the scene."

"The *scene* is my house. One of the intended victims is my son. I'm not waiting anywhere." She followed him out into bright sunlight and frigid air.

"We don't know that anyone was an intended victim. The shooting might have been a scare tactic."

"If it was, it worked. I'm scared." She climbed into the SUV, and he didn't waste energy insisting she stay behind.

If it were his son, he'd do anything to get to him.

The drive took less than five minutes, and Douglas pulled into Merry's driveway, adrenaline pumping as he eyed the shattered glass in the front window. If someone had been standing there, the gunshot could have been deadly.

Thank the Lord Keira and Tyler hadn't been injured.

Or worse.

Several neighbors huddled on the sidewalk, and Ida Sanderson stood on the porch talking to Owen.

Probably not just talking.

Ida had a strong will and a reputation for getting what she wanted. More than likely, she wanted to go in the house. A reasonable request since the Cape Cod had been in her family for generations. Now, though, it was a crime scene, and she'd have to stay out until Owen and Douglas were finished gathering evidence.

Merry was exiting the SUV and racing across the yard before Douglas put the vehicle in Park. He followed, jogging up the porch steps, Ida's voice following him into the foyer.

She was definitely on a rant, her strident demand to be allowed inside the house carrying on the frigid air. She wouldn't get her way.

Keira was waiting for him. "Where is Tyler?"

"Upstairs in the back bedroom. I figured that was the safest place for him. Merry just went up."

"You're sure he's okay?" Douglas glanced into the living room. Glass blanketed the sofa and floor, and he imagined Tyler sitting there, playing with a car, sharp projectiles suddenly showering around him.

"Not a scratch on him. We were both in the kitchen when it happened."

"Did you get a look at the car?"

"An SUV. Dark blue. No license plate."

"Sounds like the vehicle Merry saw last night. How about the driver? Did you see him?"

"By the time I got outside, the car was too far way for me to see the driver. One of the neighbors might have, though."

"We'll take their statements. See what they have to say."

"What they're going to say is that we should be doing more to stop the crime wave that seems to be sweeping Fitzgerald Bay."

"It's hardly a crime wave, Keira."

"Those aren't my words. They're Ida's."

"That doesn't surprise me."

"Yeah, well, we can't afford to have her grumbling to the community. Not when people are already speculating about Olivia's murder and pointing fingers at Charles." She frowned, shoving down her hat on straight black hair.

"No one is pointing fingers at anyone."

"Of course they are. Fortunately, there's no proof that

Charles was involved in Olivia's death. If there was, certain people around town would be demanding his arrest."

She was right.

Douglas knew it, but he didn't like it. Didn't like that the community he'd grown up in, the community he loved would turn away from a man who'd served them so loyally. "Charles has plenty of friends in the community. He's also got us. He'll be fine."

"He'll be better once we find Olivia's murderer." Keira walked into the living room and used a gloved hand to lift a bullet from the floor. "I'm thinking that might be the same person who fired this."

"Don't assume things, Keira. We need facts, not conjecture." He took the bullet. High caliber handgun. It could easily have gone through siding and drywall.

Had murder been the intention?

Or had the shooter been trying to instill a sense of fear, perhaps convey a warning?

Without knowing the motivation, it was impossible to predict the perpetrator's next move. If they couldn't predict it, they couldn't stop it.

And, Douglas *did* plan to stop it.

One young woman was already dead. He wouldn't let another be killed.

Whether Merry wanted to or not, she was going to have to start talking. Not just about Olivia. About everything. Somewhere in the secrets she'd been keeping were the answers he needed to keep her safe. All Douglas had to do was convince her to share them.

NINE

Merry's heart pounded frantically as she hugged Tyler close. He could have been killed, and it would have been her fault for staying too long in one place. Three years of running and another on constant alert had left her worn out and on edge. Fitzgerald Bay had been a balm to her frazzled nerves. She'd soaked up the easy small-town pace, let herself believe that four years was enough time.

Let herself believe it because she'd wanted to, not because it was true.

She hugged Tyler a little tighter, her mind racing with all the things that needed to be done.

Pack a few of Tyler's toys.

Leave a note for Ida.

Kiss goodbye all her dreams of settling down and settling in.

They'd be on the run again, and this time, Merry wouldn't stop running, wouldn't get complacent, wouldn't ever stop believing that their lives depended on staying one step ahead of the danger that followed.

"You're smotherin' me, Mommy." Tyler pushed against her chest, and she eased her hold.

"Sorry, sweetie." She brushed soft black hair from his forehead, kissed his chubby cheek, her heart clenching hard with love.

She'd never planned to be a single mother. As a matter of fact, she'd spent the six years after the car accident that had killed her parents imagining what her life would be like when her younger brother and sister were finally grown and out of the house. She'd planned to date, fall in love, get married. Children were a part of that dream, but they would come after the big wedding and romantic honeymoon.

That's the way she had wanted it.

The way she had thought God wanted it.

And then Nicole had walked into her classroom, and everything had changed.

Take him and run. I'll come as soon as I can.

Only Nicole hadn't been able to come. Not then. Not ever.

Merry shuddered, opening her closet and pulling out the overnight bag she kept there. Packed with a few of her things and a few of Tyler's, it contained only what they'd need to travel to the next place. Everything else had to be left behind. Clothes, books, the dishes she'd bought from the thrift store a few days after she'd arrived in town, the house she'd grown to love.

Her job.

Her friends.

She blinked rapidly, forcing back tears that she wouldn' shed. She'd grab the money and the bankbook out of the closet after the police left, pack some snacks and drinks and a few toys. Then she and Tyler would get in the car and they'd drive away from the beautiful little town she had thought she could make their forever home.

"Please, Lord, keep us safe and help me find just the right place for us to settle down again."

"Are you praying, Mommy?" Tyler bounced on her bed and she didn't have the heart to tell him to stop. He had friends, too. A preschool he loved. A yard and toys and a room that he wouldn't want to leave behind. When he'd been an infant, a baby, a toddler, it had been easy to move from place to place, but the older Tyler got, the more reluctant he became to leave people and places behind.

One day, he'd ask her why they moved all the time. She wasn't sure what she'd tell him. Didn't know how she could explain the horrible circumstances that had led to their nomadic existence. Didn't know how she could explain the truth about his parents. He'd only asked about his father, and he'd easily accepted that he simply didn't have one. One day, though, he'd demand the truth.

"Are you, Mommy? Are you praying?" Tyler tugged her hand, and she pushed the worries away. There'd be time to think of the answers she'd give *after* she and Tyler were safely away.

"Yes. I'm praying."

"What are you praying about? 'Cause, I'm gonna pray, too."

She thought about refusing to answer but keeping things from Tyler wouldn't change them or make them any easier for him to bear. "We're going on a road trip, and I was asking God to keep us safe."

"Are we coming back?" He stopped bouncing, his black eyes narrowing as he waited for the answer. He knew, of course. They'd moved a dozen times in his short life, and he understood that road trips meant never returning.

"Why don't you go in your room and pick a couple of your favorite toys to bring? Nothing big, though, okay?"

"Joe invited me to his party, remember? It's in two weeks and one day," he said, and Merry's heart broke just a little more.

"I remember. Go pick your toys." She opened the door,

praying he wouldn't put up a fuss, and walked straight into Douglas.

"Whoa! Careful." His hands cupped her shoulders, holding her steady, his warmth seeping through her coat and T-shirt. She wanted to step into his arms, absorb even more of his heat, but doing that would be almost as much of a mistake as staying in Fitzgerald Bay had been.

The easy way is for you to tell me everything. All the stuff that you're so determined to keep hidden. Whatever it is, I'll help you deal with it.

His words had terrified and tempted her.

She was so tired of going it alone, so tired of only having herself to depend on. If Owen hadn't walked into Douglas's office with the news of the shooting, Merry wasn't sure what she would have said.

Everything?

Nothing?

"Sorry. I wasn't expecting you there. Ty, go on in your room and do what I said." She stepped back and allowed Tyler to pass, hoping she was blocking Douglas's view of the room and the overnight bag.

"Ida wanted you to know that she's already called a company to come repair the window. They should be here in the next hour." He studied her face, his eyes deep, calm blue, and she felt it building up again. The need to confess everything. To tell him the truth about Tyler, about their years of running, about the lie she'd been living.

The need to let him do what he'd promised.

Help her deal with things.

She swallowed back words she couldn't say and tried to smile. "That's Ida for you. Always on top of things."

"She's been that way for as long as I've known her. That quality must make her a good landlady."

"It does. Can you tell her I'll be down in a minute?"

She started to close the bedroom door, but he slammed his palm into the wood.

"We need to talk, Merry."

"I'll be down in a minute," she repeated, and he shook his head.

"We need to talk now. Not in a minute. Not in ten minutes. Not tomorrow. Now."

"Okay." She edged into the hallway, shut the door. "What do you want to discuss?"

"How about we go down to the kitchen? I could use a cup of coffee."

"Sure." But she didn't want to go to the kitchen, didn't want to have a conversation, didn't want to do anything but pack up and head out.

She followed him downstairs anyway, turned on the coffeepot, inhaling deeply as the pungent scent of coffee filled the room.

Seconds ticked by, then minutes, and Douglas didn't say anything, just watched as she poured the coffee, handed him a mug, grabbed a pop from the fridge.

She took a long swallow, praying she wouldn't choke on it.

Finally, she couldn't stand the silence any longer. "You said we needed to talk."

"I meant, *you* need to talk. I need to listen."

"Oh."

That's it. All she could come up with.

Because, he was right. She *did* need to talk.

But talking could cost her everything, and she had to stay silent.

Had to.

"That's not a very good start to the conversation." He sipped coffee, eyeing her over the rim of the mug.

"I don't know what you want me to say."

"No? Then, maybe I do need to talk, and *you* need to listen. Last night, someone tried to get in your house. Today, that same person shot through your front window. Do you know what would have happened if Tyler had been standing near the window?"

Did she know?

She couldn't forget.

"I know."

"Then you understand how serious this is."

"How could I not? My son means everything to me. wouldn't do anything to jeopardize his safety."

"Yet, you're still holding back. Still not telling me everything I need to know to help you."

"If you want to help me, let me get a few hours of sleep. I'm exhausted." She tried to nudge him into leaving, but Douglas leaned in, his finger sweeping the delicate flesh beneath her eye.

"You have dark circles. Maybe you'll sleep better if you share your troubles. Tell me what's going on, and I'll do whatever is necessary to keep you and Tyler safe." His voice was as soft as a summer breeze, the words gentle and easy and undemanding.

"I can't."

"You *won't*." He tucked a lock of hair behind her ear, his touch gentle and more welcome than it should have been.

"It's not—" Her cell phone rang, and she grabbed it, so thankful for the distraction she could have cried. "Hello?"

"It's Mack. Is everything okay?" Her brother sounded like he always did, serious and just a little worried.

"Everything is fine." She lied. Again.

Another lie on top of all the others, and she felt sick with them, burdened with their weight.

"Are you sure? You sound upset."

"I'm just tired."

"The job is wearing you out, huh?"

"Yes." She glanced at Douglas, walked a few steps away, hoping he couldn't hear her brother's words.

"How's the little guy?"

"Great."

"That's what you always say."

"Because it's true."

"Well, if everything is okay, why didn't you return my call?"

"Your call?" She glanced at the answering machine, saw the flashing light.

"I called yesterday and left a message on your voice mail. Are you sure you're all right?"

"I think I should be asking you that. You never call me on the weekend." As a matter of fact, he almost never called. Too many years and too many lies stood between them, and Merry knew he felt those things acutely. Like their sister, Danielle, he had given up trying to maintain the close relationship he'd once had with Merry.

She missed that. Missed what might have been if she could have told him the truth about Tyler and their constant need to move. Told the truth about why she only gave a P.O. box in different cities and never a street address.

Just plain told the truth.

"I wanted to touch base. And, actually," he hesitated, and Merry knew he had something big to say.

"What?"

"I proposed to Emily, yesterday. She said yes."

"That's wonderful news, Mack! I'm so happy for you."

"The wedding is going to be in December. We want you to come."

"To Boston?" She realized what she'd done as soon as

the question slipped out. Given Douglas a piece of information she shouldn't have.

She didn't glance his way. Prayed he hadn't heard.

But he had.

She knew he had.

"Yeah. You can make it can't you?"

"Of course I can." But she couldn't. No matter how much she wanted to. Anywhere but Boston.

"I can't tell you how happy I am to hear that!"

"I love you, Mack. I wouldn't miss out on it for the world."

They chatted for a few more minutes, Mack's excitement over his engagement ringing through the phone. Finally, he said goodbye, and Merry hung up, turning to face Douglas again.

"Boyfriend?" he asked, and Merry almost laughed. Boyfriend? Having one now would mean lie after lie after lie told to someone she should only ever be honest with. Besides if she'd been willing to date someone long enough to call him her boyfriend, she would have continued to go out with Douglas. The thought made her blush.

No. Dating was out of the question.

Another lonely truth of the life she led.

"My brother."

"I didn't realize you had other family. I thought it was just you and Tyler."

It was, because she couldn't pull her brother and sister into her troubles and because she couldn't tell them the truth about how Tyler had come into her life.

"I have a sister and brother. Our parents died in a car accident when I was eighteen. I took care of them until they graduated from college."

"You must be really close."

"We are." But not as close as they used to be.

"So why are you here? Why aren't you living near your family?"

"People move away from family all the time."

"That's a statement. Not an answer."

"There is no answer. I just…moved away after they went to college."

"Away from Boston?"

"Just away," she said too forcefully, and heat spread up her cheeks.

She did not want to look him in the eye and lie.

She didn't want to keep covering one lie with another and another.

She just wanted him to accept what she said and go away.

But he wouldn't.

Douglas wasn't that kind of guy.

"Merry—"

"I need to get some air." She shoved past him, running across the kitchen and out into the backyard, inhaling huge gulps of frigid air. If not for Tyler, she would have kept running, but Tyler needed her more than she needed to be free of Douglas. More than she needed to be free of the heavy burden of guilt she carried every moment of every day.

She skidded to a stop in the middle of the yard, dropped down onto one of the old vinyl swings. She'd planned to fix the swing set in the spring. Put new seats on the swings, clean the slide and put a sandbox next to it. She'd been saving money for months with that in mind. She'd be using that money for a deposit on another home instead.

Elbows on her knees, she stared at the blanket of snow beneath her feet, so tired she wasn't sure she'd ever get up. Tired of running, tired of hiding, tired of partial truths and half lies and always looking over her shoulder.

Just plain tired.

But at least she and Tyler were alive.

That was more than Olivia had. It was more than Nicole had.

Alive with a son she loved and siblings who cared.

It was enough, and she would be thankful for it.

TEN

He needed a new approach.

Obviously, pushing Merry was only making her run, and having her run wasn't what he wanted.

What he wanted was the truth. All of it. Not the little pieces she kept feeding him.

He pulled off his coat as he walked across the backyard and dropped it onto her shoulders. "You're going to freeze out here."

"Thanks, but now *you're* going to be cold." She offered a half smile, her lips nearly colorless.

"Neither of us will be cold if we go back inside." He sat on an old swing, wincing as the rusted chains creaked under his weight. "I don't think this swing set is made for someone my size."

"I don't think it's meant for someone my size, either," she responded, pushing against the ground with her feet.

"*Your* size? A stiff wind could blow you away."

Her eyes widened, and she laughed, the sound spilling out into the quiet yard, a tinge of color staining her pale cheeks.

"That's better."

"What?" She hooked a lock of red-gold hair behind her ear, and he wanted to reach out and touch the silky strands that fell around her shoulders. She compelled him in a way he couldn't explain, drew him in and made him want to stick close.

"You've got some color back in your cheeks."

"Cold will do that to a person. Sorry for running out like that. I guess I'm a little overwhelmed with everything that's happened. The past twenty-four hours have been really stressful, and you…well, I can't answer your questions. I don't have any answers to give you."

"I think you have answers. I think you just don't want to share them."

"What if you're right? What if there *are* things I don't want to share? What does it matter? It's nothing to do with Olivia or her murder. I can promise you that." She shifted uncomfortably, her feet digging into the snow, her head bent so that he couldn't read her expression.

"Finding Olivia's murderer isn't the only thing I'm concerned about. I told you that I'm concerned about Tyler. I'm concerned about you."

"You don't have to be. We've been going it alone for four years, and we've been just fine."

"Someone is hunting you, Merry. Stalking your house. Shooting at your windows. I'd say that's a far cry from fine."

"I'm cold. I'm tired. I need to get some rest. Can we finish this tomorrow?" She didn't acknowledge his comment, didn't pretend to answer it.

"Sure." He tugged her upright, led her to the house, acted like he really thought they'd pick up the conversation the next day.

Only, he didn't think she planned to be around. He'd seen a small suitcase sitting on the floor in her room. She planned to run.

No way was he going to let her. Running wouldn't solve

her problems. It wouldn't keep her safe. She needed to stay in Fitzgerald Bay, stay close to people who knew her and cared about her.

And he did care.

Too much to accept her lies and cover-ups.

If she wasn't willing to tell him what he wanted to know, he'd simply do what he'd threatened. A background check. He'd taken her fingerprints. If she'd come to Fitzgerald Bay to hide from the law, he'd know it soon enough, but he didn't believe that was the case. She was hiding from something else. Someone else?

"I need to check on Tyler." She hurried into the house, and he let her go, knowing he'd get little else out of her.

He'd let her try to make a run for it.

Maybe when he caught her fleeing and stopped her, she'd be more willing to tell him what she was running from.

"Douglas!" Owen rounded the side of the house, his dark hair mussed.

"Right here. What's up?" He walked to his brother's side, trying to push thoughts of Merry out of his head.

"We're finished collecting evidence. Keira is bringing what little we found to the station."

"Are you heading back there, too?"

"No. I'm going to see Granddad and try to talk some sense into him. At least, that's what Dad wants me to do."

"Some sense into him about what? His retirement?"

"Dad doesn't think he's ready."

"In this instance, Dad's opinion doesn't matter. Granddad has been working hard for a long time. He deserves to retire." Douglas walked to Owen's car, his gaze drawn to the house's second-story window. Was Merry packing? Did she really think she'd be able to leave?

There he went, thinking about her again.

Had he really thought he could push her out of his thoughts?

She'd been there since the first day he'd seen her. Lunches together hadn't changed that. Her secrets hadn't changed that.

"You don't have to convince me," Owen said. "It's Dad who's having issues with it. Maybe you've been too caught up in the murder investigation to notice, but he hasn't been himself since Granddad's announcement."

"I was thinking Dad hadn't been the same since Olivia's body was discovered."

"They both happened the same day, but Olivia wasn't family. Granddad is."

"So is Charles." Douglas didn't have to say any more. Owen had heard the whispers, and he knew exactly why the family had reason to be concerned.

"I guess that's reason enough for Dad to be upset. Whatever the case, he wants me to talk to Granddad, and I'm going to do it. Don't be surprised if he asks you to do the same."

Douglas nodded. "Thanks for the heads-up."

"Are you planning to work late tonight?"

"Yes, and I'll probably be at the office early tomorrow morning. I have to take some time off in the afternoon, but I'll be back in the evening." And he'd be searching. For Olivia's killer. For Merry's secrets.

"Take some time off from what? You're not scheduled to work."

"We're in the middle of a murder investigation, and there's no way I'm *not* going to be at the office. If I hadn't agreed to meet Aunt Vanessa for tea—"

"Tea?" Owen laughed as they walked out to his car.

"Yeah. Tea."

"You know what that means, right?"

"It means she's going to have a half-dozen eligible bach-elorettes waiting for me at Connolly's Catch." And that made Douglas want to stay as far away from his uncle and aunt's restaurant as he could. Unfortunately, he loved his aunt too much to keep sidestepping her invitations.

"It means that she wants to see you happily married. Like she is." Owen smirked, his eyes flashing with humor.

"She wants to see *all* of us happily married, but I'm not in the mood for more of her matchmaking. Not with everything else that's going on." Besides, he was pretty sure he'd found his match.

"I hear you, bro. Our quiet town isn't all that quiet anymore, is it?"

"No, and I don't think that what happened today is the end of things."

Not if they couldn't find Olivia's killer.

Not if they couldn't stop whoever was stalking Merry.

"Do you think today's perp is also our murderer?" Owen asked.

"I don't know." It seemed likely, but until they had more facts, it was impossible to say.

"Does Merry have any idea why someone would shoot out the window of her house?"

"If she does, she's not saying."

"That seems odd, doesn't it? You'd think that someone in danger would be eager to provide as much information as possible in order to stay safe."

"Yeah, you'd think so," Douglas replied, glancing at the window again. Someone moved behind the curtain, and he was sure it was Merry. Was she peeking out, hoping they'd leave quickly so she could go?

"Have you run a background check on her?"

"I took her fingerprints today. We're checking to see if she's in the system. I don't think she will be."

"But?"

"I think she's running from something, and I think there's a lot she hasn't told me."

"Do you think she's a killer?" Owen asked, and Douglas met his eyes, saw the intensity and focus that made him such a good police officer.

"No."

"She has an alibi for the night of Olivia's murder?"

"Her neighbors insist she was home all night. I have various witnesses who saw her car in the driveway during the time the murder took place."

"They could be wrong."

"Merry doesn't have a mean bone in her body, Owen. Even if she didn't have an alibi, I wouldn't believe she was a murderer."

"Too bad. I was hoping we had a suspect."

"Like I said, Merry isn't a murderer," he said forcefully, and Owen raised an eyebrow.

"You're awfully protective when it comes to Merry."

"I'm just making sure we don't pin a crime on an innocent person."

"Merry isn't the only innocent person who might be implicated in this," Owen pointed out.

"I know, but I'm not going to toss Merry to the wolves to throw them off Charles's scent."

"You know that's the last thing I'd want to have happen. But I also don't want to bypass a person of interest because she has a pretty face and a sweet smile."

"I think you know that I would never let a pretty face or a sweet smile sway me," Douglas responded without heat. Owen sounded as weary as Douglas felt, and for good reason. The law might dictate that a person was innocent until proven guilty, but in the minds of some of Fitzgerald Bay's citizens, Charles was guilty until proven innocent. Without evidence to show that someone else had committed the crime, the whispers would continue and the gossip would spread.

"Sorry. I didn't mean that the way it sounded. I know the kind of police officer you are. I know the kind of *man* you are. I just want to make sure we're not overlooking anything."

"You and me both."

"Let me know if anything comes up when you run Merry's fingerprints, okay?"

"Will do."

"I'd better go. Granddad's expecting me. See you tomorrow." Owen got in his car, and Douglas watched as he drove away.

Dusk had already fallen, draping the landscape in purple-blue light. Another day passed with no name or face to put to Olivia's murderer, and Douglas felt the weight of that as he walked back to Merry's house.

He didn't bother knocking, just opened the door and stepped into the tiny foyer, his gaze jumping to movement at the top of the stairs.

Merry froze as their eyes met, her fists tightening around the boxes she clutched. Crackers. Cookies. What looked like a package of cheese.

"Didn't your mother teach you to knock?" she asked, her voice breathless and filled with anxiety.

"Didn't yours teach you not to bring food into your bedroom?"

She looked down at the food, frowned as if she weren't quite sure how it had gotten in her hands. "It's cold downstairs, and Tyler was hungry. I'm bringing him a snack."

"He must be really hungry if you're planning to feed him an entire box of crackers and a box of cookies."

"I'm hungry, too." She set the boxes and cheese on a small table that stood against the wall and walked down the stairs. "I thought you were gone."

"Obviously."

"What's that supposed to mean?" Her eyes were wide with fear, but she seemed determined to pretend that she really had been bringing Tyler a snack.

"I don't think you'd have started packing to leave if you knew I was still outside."

"I'm not—"

"You are, but if you want to stay safe, you'd better follow a few simple rules. First, keep your cell phone on you at all times. Do you have it?"

She frowned but pulled it from her purse.

Before she could shove it into her pocket, he snagged it.

"What are you doing?" She made a grab for it, but she was a head shorter with arms to match, and he held it out of her reach.

"Adding my phone number to your contact list."

"There's no need—"

"There's every need. I live a few blocks away. If something happens and you need help quickly, call 9-1-1 and then call me. I can be here in minutes."

"Douglas—"

"Second rule. Keep your doors and windows locked and your alarm on."

"I always do that."

Douglas's backward glance at the front door he had just walked through discounted that statement. "Third and final rule. Don't leave town."

We'd like to send you two free books to introduce you to the Love Inspired® Suspense series. These books are worth over $10, are yours to keep absolutely FREE! We'll even send you two wonderful surprise gifts. You can't lose!

Each of your books is filled with riveting inspirational suspense featuring Christian characters facing challenges to their faith...and their lives!

Visit us at
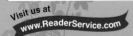
www.ReaderService.com

GET 2 FREE BOOKS!

HURRY!
Return this card today to get 2 FREE Books and 2 FREE Bonus Gifts!

YES! Please send me the **2 FREE Love Inspired® Suspense books** and **2 FREE gifts** for which I qualify. I understand that I am under no obligation to purchase anything further, as explained on the back of this card.

PLACE FREE GIFTS SEAL HERE

❏ I prefer the regular-print edition
123/323 IDL FMSG

❏ I prefer the larger-print edition
110/310 IDL FMSG

FIRST NAME   LAST NAME

ADDRESS

APT.#   CITY

STATE/PROV.   ZIP/POSTAL CODE

Offer limited to one per household and not applicable to series that subscriber is currently receiving.
Your Privacy—The Reader Service is committed to protecting your privacy. Our Privacy Policy is available online at www.ReaderService.com or upon request from the Reader Service. We make a portion of our mailing list available to reputable third parties that offer products we believe may interest you. If you prefer that we not exchange your name with third parties, or if you wish to clarify or modify your communication preferences, please visit us at www.ReaderService.com/consumerschoice or write to us at Reader Service Preference Service, P.O. Box 9062, Buffalo, NY 14269. Include your complete name and adddress.

BUSINESS REPLY MAIL

FIRST-CLASS MAIL   PERMIT NO. 717   BUFFALO, NY

POSTAGE WILL BE PAID BY ADDRESSEE

THE READER SERVICE

PO BOX 1341

BUFFALO NY 14240-8571

NO POSTAGE
NECESSARY
IF MAILED
IN THE
UNITED STATES

She froze, her entire body going rigid. "Why would I leave town?"

"Good question. Maybe you can answer it for both of us."

"I need to get back to Tyler. What happened today scared him, and he doesn't want me far from his side." She headed up the stairs, but he grabbed the belt loop of her jeans.

"What you need is someone you can trust."

"And that's you?"

"Yeah. It is."

"Douglas—"

"When you're ready to talk, give me a call. And, remember what I said, don't leave town." He walked out into bitter cold, letting the air sweep over him, fill his lungs, clear his head.

Life in Fitzgerald Bay had a predictable rhythm and an easy flow that he'd always loved. While his high-school peers had talked about heading to big cities after graduation, he'd dreamed of staying exactly where he was, working for the police force, raising a family in the sleepy little fishing town where he'd grown up.

Things had turned out the way he'd wanted.

Except in one area of his life.

There'd been no wedding, no kids, nothing but a series of girlfriends who had been nice enough.

Nice enough wasn't good enough.

Douglas knew enough about love to know that.

He'd rather be single than settle for anything less than the kind of relationship his parents had had. That's why he'd backed out of the dating scene, tried to avoid the matchmaking efforts of his friends and family. He'd decided he'd be content with what he had and not keep asking God for something more.

Merry had changed all that. He'd seen her, and he'd known he couldn't resist her smile, couldn't deny himself the opportunity to get to know her. Two dates, and he'd wanted so much more. He'd wanted to memorize her smile and her laughter, wanted to know every part of who she was, but she'd turned him away. Despite the way he'd felt, he'd let her, because pushing for something she didn't want wasn't his style. No more lunches. No dinners. No more going into the Reading Nook to see if Merry was there.

He'd done what she'd wanted and left her alone.

Now he was going to do what he wanted.

He was going to stick close, keep an eye on Merry and Tyler, keep them safe. And, when it was over and they were out of danger, he was going to do what he should have done from the very beginning. Learn every part of who Merry was.

Including every one of her secrets.

ELEVEN

Stay.

Go.

Merry wasn't sure what was right anymore.

What you need is someone you can trust.

That's what Douglas had said, and he was right.

She *did* need someone to trust, but trusting would mean putting Tyler's life in someone else's hands, and she couldn't do that.

She shoved toys into an oversize duffle, tucked the crackers, cookies and cheese on top of them and zipped the bag.

That was it.

They were ready to go.

She carried the duffle to the front door, set it next to the overnight case, her heart heavy with what she was about to do.

An image of Douglas flashed through her mind. Deep black hair and vivid blue eyes. Compassion and strength and something indefinable, but so compelling, she'd almost told him what he wanted to know.

More than once.

And that scared her.

Even if she could make herself believe that staying in

Fitzgerald Bay was safe, she knew that staying around Douglas wasn't.

The wind howled, carrying in another storm. She needed to get out of town before it hit. The station wagon didn't do well in snow, and if she didn't leave soon, she wouldn't be able to leave until the storm blew over.

That wasn't an option.

No matter how heavyhearted she felt, no matter how much she'd rather stay, leaving was the only choice.

She hurried into her room, pulled the bankbook, the journal and the cash from their hiding place.

Tyler's inheritance. All of it. One day, she'd have to tell him the truth about his beginnings. She'd have to tell him about Nicole. When she did, she'd pull out the journal and the bankbook. Until then, she kept them hidden safely away. Hidden like so many other things.

Like the truth.

Merry traced the numbers and letters carved into the front of the journal's cover. Nicole's doing, but Merry had never figured out what they meant. Maybe they were a secret message for Tyler. If so, she hoped he would have an easier time deciphering them than she had.

She sighed, dropping the journal and bankbook into her purse, then pulling out cash from the stack of bills and shoving the remainder in her bag. Her emergency fund taken from the money she'd received after her parents' house had gone to escrow. She kept it close rather than in a bank. Cautious. Careful. Prepared.

But that didn't mean she wanted to leave.

Hot tears clogged her throat as she scribbled a note on a piece of paper, hurried down to the kitchen to leave it and the cash on the table. A few months' rent for Ida to make up for leaving unexpectedly.

But they'd been friends, and she was leaving without

saying goodbye. Leaving forever with no intention of ever contacting Ida again.

Leaving Fitzgerald Bay was almost more difficult than leaving Boston had been. Almost more difficult than leaving her childhood home, her siblings, the person she used to be. Because, after years of running, she'd finally felt at home, finally felt as if she was safe. That had been a heady feeling.

While it lasted.

But she wasn't safe anymore.

She walked into Tyler's room, her pulse racing as she touched his shoulder. "Buddy? Time to get up. We have to go."

He rolled onto his belly, buried his head deep into the pillow.

"Come on, Ty. Up you go." She tugged off the covers, tickled his feet.

"Don't want to." He whined but sat up, wrapping his arms around Merry's waist and pressing his head against her stomach.

"It's going to be fun." She kept her voice cheerful and bright, hoping to convince herself and him.

"Staying here is fun. Going to Mark's party is fun."

"You'll make new friends."

"I want my old friends." He scowled, his dark hair falling down into his eyes.

"You can have new friends *and* old friends."

"We're not coming back, though. I want to come back."

"Maybe we will." It's what she'd said every time they left.

"Okay." His sigh was like an old man's, and guilt piled upon guilt as she helped him dress, grabbed a few more items of clothing from his dresser and led him down the stairs.

She buttoned his coat, pulled a knit hat over his soft black hair, kissed his cheek. "You're the best four-year-old boy I know. You know that, Tyler William O'Leary?"

"You're the best mommy I know. You know that, Mommy?" He threw himself into her arms, and she blinked back tears. This wasn't what she wanted for her son, leaving a home they both loved in the middle of the night.

It wasn't what she wanted for herself.

What you need is someone you can trust.

Douglas's words seemed to hang in the air as she disarmed the alarm and unlocked the door. She'd been asking God for help since she'd fled Boston, begging Him to give her a way out that wouldn't cost her Tyler. Maybe Douglas was that way. Maybe he was the help she'd been praying for.

Or, maybe he was the beginning of the end.

As soon as he realized she'd fled, he'd try to track her down. She'd have to move quickly to keep a step ahead. Change her name again. Get a new car, new identification. New life.

And, she'd have to change Tyler's name.

This would be the first time she'd have to tell him that. How would she explain that to a four-year-old?

Merry stooped to help Tyler with his mittens, pulling them up under his sleeve, her thumb brushing the raised mark, the catalyst that had sent her world into a tailspin. A brand seared into the flesh of a newborn baby.

Please, take him. I'll follow as soon as I can. If I can't... you have to keep him safe. Promise me you will.

Nicole had spoken the words through swollen, bleeding lips, her face puffy from tears and swollen from the beating she'd received from Tyrone Rodriguez. Her boyfriend. Tyler's father.

Merry shoved away the memory. If she dwelled in the past, she couldn't live in the moment, and living in the moment was the only way to survive.

"Okay, buddy. We're out of here."

"Yep. Out of here!" Tyler's cheerful good humor had returned and he skipped out the door, completely oblivious to the danger that had been hunting him his entire life.

Merry unlocked the station wagon, urged Tyler to hurry into his car seat, her pulse pounding frantically in her ears, the howling wind and frigid air shivering through her.

"Hurry, sweetie."

She was sure she felt eyes tracking her movements as she tossed the suitcase and duffle into the backseat, hurried around the car and into the driver's seat.

Her hands shook as she shoved the keys into the ignition, praying desperately that the car would start. Old and fickle, it protested the cold weather, sputtering to life in a series of short, sharp sounds that were sure to bring neighbors to their windows.

Just go!

She stepped on the gas, pulling out of the driveway and onto the street, her hands sweaty on the cold steering wheel, her body humming with nerves.

She had to get out of town, get on the interstate highway, drive and drive until she couldn't drive anymore. Eventually, she'd find a place to settle again. Eventually, another town would feel like home.

"Where we goin' this time, Mommy?"

"Somewhere warm?" she suggested, her mouth so dry, her throat so tight the words sounded raspy and harsh.

"Cold. Like this place."

"Okay. Somewhere cold." She glanced in her rearview mirror. One last look at the house they'd spent a year living in. One last look, only the house wasn't the only thing she saw.

A man stood in the middle of the road. Tall. Blond. Very, very thin. Something in his hands. A gun!

A loud pop startled a shriek out of her, and she barely managed to keep the car on the road as it pulled to the left, bumping along the pavement.

A blown tire.

Pop!

Bump.

Pull.

The car shimmied and jerked, and she slammed on the brakes, saw *him* in her rearview mirror. Loping toward the car, long legs eating up the ground, face hidden in shadows, the gun aimed at the back of the station wagon.

No!

Please, God, protect Tyler.

She stepped on the gas pedal with all her strength, the car shooting forward as a third pop dragged it to the right and into a tangle of bushes that lined Old Man Silverman's yard.

Please, God. Please!

The car stalled there, the old vehicle absolutely refusing to start again.

Please!

She grabbed her cell phone, dialed 9-1-1, Douglas's words ringing in her ears as she shouted her situation and location, begged the dispatcher to send help quickly.

Don't leave town.

Stay in the house.

Call if you need me.

"We have patrol cars en route. Stay on the phone, ma'am." But Merry tossed the phone onto the dashboard, turned to Tyler.

"Listen to me. Unbuckle your seat belt. We're going to play hide and go seek in the dark just like you've always wanted to. When I say run, I want you to open the door and jump right into those big bushes."

"You hide with me, Mommy!" He'd already gotten out of his seat, and he scrambled into her lap, clung to her the way he had when he'd been a toddler.

The light came on outside the Silverman's house and the front door opened.

"You're a brave boy, remember? You're going to run into those bushes, and then you're going to hide in every bush you can find all the way to Mr. Silverman's front door. Mr. Silverman is standing right there." She glanced in the rearview mirror. A hundred yards away, the figure darted behind a thick oak tree. Gone, but not for good.

She opened the door. "You have to run, okay, Ty?"

"Mommy, no!" Tyler clasped her shoulders, refusing to release his hold.

"Honey, go! Now!" She dragged his hands from her shoulders, nudged him into the thick scratchy shrubs, her heart breaking into a million pieces as he wailed in fear.

All her fault.

If anything happened to Tyler...

She grabbed her purse, jumped out of the station wagon, searching the darkness for signs of the gunman. Lights flashed on the snow-encrusted ground and footsteps sounded behind her.

She turned, swinging the purse blindly, terror fueling her.

"Merry, it's me, Douglas." His hands cupped her shoulders.

Douglas.

She looked up into his face. "Thank God!"

"I told you to stay inside. You should have listened," he growled.

"Tyler. I need to get him." She tried to move away. Wanted to stop looking up into his angry eyes, but he held her arms, his hands light and warm around her biceps. "He's at the Silverman's."

"I told you not to leave town, Merry. *This* is why. It's not safe for you to be wandering around without protection."

He was right. Tyler could have been killed.

One of the bullets could have gone through the back window, slammed into Tyler's little body.

Douglas walked her to the Silverman's house and she rang the doorbell, knowing that her need to save her son had nearly cost his life.

Sirens screamed behind her, more police officers arriving as Mr. Silverman opened his door, scowled and gestured for her to enter.

She stepped into the foyer, wincing as Tyler's piercing cries filled her ears. She followed the sound into a large living room. Tyler sat on the floor, tears streaming down his face. He reached for her as she moved close, his hands grasping and holding as she lifted him.

"It's okay, sweetie. Everything is okay," she whispered.

But it wasn't okay.

She'd tried to run. Failed.

She didn't think Douglas would give her a chance to try again. Didn't think she dared try again. Not with danger so close. She buried her face in Tyler's soft hair, inhaled the scent of baby shampoo and winter.

The problem was, staying meant saying goodbye to everything she'd worked so hard to protect, everything she loved.

She couldn't do that.

Wouldn't.

"It's okay," she said again, as much to comfort herself as to comfort Tyler, but the words rang hollow in her ears, and all she could do was pray they were true as she listened to the sirens and waited for Douglas to come.

TWELVE

She'd run. Just like he'd thought she would, and if Douglas hadn't been parked at the corner of her street, staking out her house, waiting for her to do what he'd expected, she'd be dead.

He scowled, anger and adrenaline sweeping through him as he raced across Jason and Laura Hooper's backyard and out into the adjacent street, running in the direction the perp had gone.

Nothing.

No one.

That's exactly what Douglas had expected, but not what he'd wanted. Turning on the cruiser's emergency lights had kept the gunman from firing again, but it had also warned him away.

It had taken a few seconds too long to drive from the end of the street to the old station wagon, and the perp had slipped through the shadows as Douglas jumped out of the SUV and gave chase. He'd known when he heard an engine roar to life, that the perp had escaped. Known it but hadn't wanted it to be true.

Frustrated, Douglas took off his hat, raked a hand through his hair.

"Hey, Douglas! Any sign of the perp?" His brother Ryan ran toward him, and Douglas shook his head.

"He had a vehicle parked on this street. I heard him drive away as I was running through the Hoopers' yard."

"He was after Merry?"

"Yeah." Douglas flashed his light on the ground, following a trail of footprints to the curb. "This is where he parked."

He looked back the way they'd come, saw Merry's little Cape Cod.

"He had a good view of Merry's house," Ryan said, easily following the train of Douglas's thoughts.

"He was probably waiting for an opportunity to strike again." And Merry had given it to him by leaving her house without protection, walking out into danger without anyone around to help her.

If he hadn't been there...

An image of Merry lying in a pool of blood and little Tyler slumped in his car seat, his body riddled with bullets, filled his mind.

Douglas frowned, crouching near one of the footprints.

"I guess there was a reason why Merry and her son were leaving the house in the middle of the night." Ryan pulled out a camera and started snapping photos.

"I guess so. I plan to find out what it was once we're finished here."

"You know what I'd like to find out? How you ended up calling in the incident before Merry did."

"I was parked at the corner of the street, keeping an eye on Merry's house."

"I see."

"You see what?" Douglas asked.

"You're taking an awful lot of interest in her case."

"I'm taking an interest in all the cases that have been popping up lately."

"Good to know," Ryan said as he walked back toward Merry's house. "And seeing as how I have my hands full with the murder investigation and the bad press it's causing us, I'm happy to have you take the lead on this investigation."

"I wouldn't say we've got bad press. More like a few unhappy grumbles."

"They'll get unhappier and more plentiful if we don't find a suspect soon."

"Any luck finding someone who knows who Olivia's sweetheart is?"

Ryan shook his head. "Her cousin finally contacted us, but she couldn't tell us much more than what we already knew."

"How about Olivia's apartment? Did you turn anything up there?" Douglas stopped at the oak tree where the gunman had stood, flashing his light on the trampled earth and small spots on the ground that might have been blood.

"Nothing that will help us with the case. What's that? Blood?" Ryan studied the spots as Douglas searched the low tree branches and found what he was looking for. A broken branch with what looked like blood at its tip.

"I think our perp left a little of himself behind."

"Let's bag it. We'll send it out for blood typing and DNA matching." Ryan snapped off the branch, dropped it into an evidence bag.

Douglas's radio sputtered to life as another officer called in an abandoned SUV that matched the description of the vehicle that both Merry and Keira had seen. Douglas's pulse jumped as he met Ryan's gaze. "Sounds like our perp might be getting a little nervous. He left his ride behind."

"I'll head to the location and check things out. You can handle things here. Call in if you have any problems. Otherwise, I'll see you back at the station."

"See you there." He waited until Ryan drove away, then followed the perp's tracks again, hoping to find more evidence. Something solid that would lead him to the gunman.

The wind howled, blowing snow across the road as Douglas trekked back to Merry's car and lifted a bullet from the ground. Same caliber as the one used to shoot out her window.

Same caliber, same weapon?

They'd have to do ballistic testing to find out for sure, but Douglas was pretty confident they'd match.

A patrol car pulled up behind the station wagon, and he straightened, offering a quick wave as Hank Monroe got out and ambled over.

"I heard there was another shooting. Looks like our quiet little town is getting a lot less quiet. Most of the noise seems centered around people who work for your family. Guess the Fitzgeralds are bad luck." Hank grinned, but there wasn't any humor in his eyes. He'd been on the force for years, but Douglas didn't consider Hank a team member, and he'd rather work with anyone else. He didn't let it show, though. The Fitzgerald Bay police department was a family of sorts, and he treated all of its members with respect. Even the ones he didn't like.

"It's nothing to do with luck, Hank."

"Then what does it have to do with?"

"People who think they're God, and who believe they have the right to end another human being's life."

"True there, buddy. How many bullets were fired?"

"Three, and the guy was a pretty good shot. He fired three times and managed to take out three of Merry's tires."

"Good thing he wasn't trying to take her out."

"I'm not sure he wasn't. I have a witness to interview. Can you collect the other two bullets and look for further evidence out here?"

"In other words, freeze while you go inside where it's warm?" Hank's jovial tone didn't hide his irritation.

Douglas ignored both. "Next time, I'll take outdoor duty."

He didn't wait to hear more of Hank's subtle complaints, just left him standing near Merry's car and walked to the Silverman place. Old and stately, the Victorian home loomed over its smaller neighbors, its ornate trim and wraparound porch white and crisp in the darkness.

Douglas jogged to the mahogany door and knocked. Bill opened the door immediately, scowling again as he stepped aside and gestured impatiently for Douglas to enter. "It's about time you came and got them. Kid has been running around my living room like a mouse on a spin wheel."

"Sorry about that, Bill. We were trying to collect evidence—" *Nice of you to be so concerned,* he wanted to add.

Merry sat on the floor, her hair tumbling around her shoulders and falling into her face, her expression hidden behind thick red-gold curls.

A few feet away, Tyler moved back and forth across the room. "Bounce. Bounce. Bounce. Bounce."

"What are you doing, pal?" He put a hand on Tyler's soft black hair, imagined the same scene he had before. The sturdy little body still and lifeless, the flashing dark eyes dim and dead. His stomach clenched, his anger rising up again. He tamped it down as the little boy stopped bouncing and looked up.

"I'm a ball."

"How about you be a chair, instead?"

"A chair can't hit bad guys in the head. A ball can. Bounce. Bounce." Tyler added a growl at the end for emphasis, and Merry shifted subtly, wiping a hand down her cheek. Crying, and she should be.

He had no words of sympathy to offer. Nothing to say that would make her feel better.

He didn't want her to feel better.

He wanted her to realize just how close she'd come to losing her life, how close Tyler had come to losing his.

He wanted her to know just how serious the mistake she'd made had been.

"Tell you what. I'll take care of the bad guys, okay? You just worry about bouncing."

"*You're* gonna hit the bad guy in the head? 'Cause, we can't let him get my mommy." Tyler's eyes were big, dark pools of worry, and Douglas lifted him so they were face-to-face. Unlike Merry, the little boy had an olive complexion, his tan skin and black hair speaking of Hispanic heritage. His father must have been just as dark, and Douglas wanted to know who the man was, wanted to know what he had to do with Merry's secretive nature.

If he had anything to do with it.

"I'm going to do something better than that. I'm going to put handcuffs on him, and I'm going to put him in jail."

"You are?" Tyler wound an arm around Douglas's neck and leaned in so their noses were almost touching.

"I am."

"'Cause you're a police? That's better than a ball. Mommy said so."

"Mommy is right." He ruffled Tyler's soft hair, set him back down.

"You were fortunate tonight, Merry. Next time, you might not be." He didn't try to keep the anger from his voice, and she winced, his words striking home.

"I know." She swiped at her cheeks, the gesture quick and abrupt. "I should have listened to you. I know that, too."

"Then why didn't you?"

"Because…" She shook her head, and his frustration grew, his anger toppling over and spilling out.

"Just once, I'd like a straight answer from you. Just once, I'd like to ask a question and have you respond without hesitating and thinking it through and coming up with something that you think will protect you and Tyler. Nothing is going to protect either of you as long as I don't know what's going on."

"Bounce, bounce, bounce, bounce. Bounce!" Tyler jumped between them, his voice filling the sudden silence.

"*Ty, stop bouncing.* You're going to annoy Mr. Silverman," Merry snapped at her son, and Tyler stopped, his big eyes filling with tears.

"Sorry, Mommy."

"No. I'm sorry. I'm tired, but that's not your fault." She pulled Tyler in for a hug, her hands shaking as she patted his back. Her body shaking, and Douglas sighed, sat on the floor next to her, his arm sliding around her waist.

She stiffened, then sagged against him, her head dropping to his shoulder, silent tears still running down her cheeks. "I'm so sorry, Douglas. I don't know what I was thinking."

"You were thinking that leaving town was safer than staying. Why?" His chin brushed against her hair as he tugged her into his arms. Berries and cream. That's what she smelled like. Berries and cream and warm summer days. He wiped moisture from her cheeks, looked into her dark eyes.

She studied his face silently, her gaze like a physical touch, warm and probing, asking for something that Douglas would have been happy to give if he'd known what it was. Known what she needed.

Maybe she saw what she was looking for.

Her tension eased, the longing she felt shining out of the depth of her eyes. Longing. Desperation. The need to believe that he really could help.

"I—"

"Bounce. Bounce. Bounce. Bounce." Tyler hopped toward the living room doorway, and Merry jumped, pulling away. Physically. Mentally. Douglas could see the wall go back up, see the softness and vulnerability fade.

"Come on. Let's get you home." He lifted Tyler, deciding that the best way to interview Merry was alone. No bouncing kid. No grumpy neighbor. Just the two of them hashing things out until she told him what he wanted to know. They both thanked Mr. Silverman and headed out.

"I can carry him," Merry said, reaching for Tyler.

"You don't even look like you can carry yourself."

"I'm fi—"

"Do you have to fight me on everything?" he asked, ignoring her protest and carrying Tyler into the blustery night.

"I'm not fighting you. I'm fighting myself," Merry responded so quietly that he wasn't sure he'd heard her right.

"Why would you do that?" He glanced up and down the street, saw several officers scouring the area with flashlights. A canine unit had arrived, and the dogs had already been deployed. No way was the perp hanging around. He pressed his free hand to Merry's lower back, urging her down the porch steps and onto the sidewalk.

"Because I want things I shouldn't. Things that could destroy everything I've worked for."

"Destroy is a strong word."

"It's the one that fits." She shivered, and he pulled her close, trying to shield her from the frigid wind.

"Tell me what you've worked for."

She shook her head, and he bit down impatience and frustration. Those wouldn't help. Pushing her wouldn't help. What he needed to do was convince her.

To let go of control.

Let him into her life.

Into her secrets.

"Then tell me what you want, Merry."

"To just…"

"What?"

"Not have to go it alone anymore."

"You aren't. I'm here, and I'm going to stay."

She didn't respond, and he pressed his advantage. "I did a little research while I was waiting for you to run."

"You were waiting for me to run?"

"How do you think I got here so quickly? I was sitting at the corner of your street, waiting to stop you when you tried to leave."

"I… Thank you. You saved my life."

"I wouldn't have had to if you'd listened."

"I know."

"So, tell me what you're running from." He took house keys from her shaking hand, opened the door, Tyler's arms wrapped firmly around his neck. Solid and warm, the little boy reminded Douglas of what he'd wanted for so many years. A wife, kids, a house in the town he loved so much.

He'd thought he'd meet a local girl. A smart, funny, uncomplicated woman who'd fill the empty place in his heart, complete him in a way no one else could.

Funny. Walking into the house with Merry, feeling Tyler's sleepy body draped against his shoulder, he felt more complete than he had in a long time.

"I need to get Tyler in bed. Come on, sweetie."

"Avoiding the question won't make it go away." Douglas released his hold on the little boy, let Merry take him.

"I'm not avoiding it. I guess I just figure you already know the answer. I hoped that leaving town would keep Tyler safe. I was wrong. I'll be down in a minute." She hurried up the stairs, not giving him time to respond. She'd said as much as she planned.

He planned on getting more.

They were at an impasse, but eventually he'd break through it. Get through to her.

He walked into the kitchen, plugged in the coffeemaker, dug through cabinets until he found coffee and started a pot. A note sat on the kitchen table, a stack of money beneath it, and Douglas did what any self-respecting police officer would do, he picked up the note and read it.

Dear Ida, thank you so much for being a wonderful landlady and a great caregiver to Tyler. I can't tell you how much knowing you has meant to me. I've left a half-year's rent to make up for leaving you without a tenant. Please know that you will always be in our hearts and prayers. Best, Merry.

Six months' worth of rent?

That had to be a few thousand dollars. He lifted the stack of money, started counting it.

A thousand dollars.

Two.

Twenty-five hundred.

Three thousand.

"Don't you know better than to touch things that aren't yours?" Merry walked across the room and snatched the money and the note from his hand.

"About as well as you know not to leave money lying around where an intruder could find it." He poured coffee, handed her a cup.

"I—"

"Wanted to make sure you didn't leave Ida hanging?"

"You read the note," she accused.

"Did you think I wouldn't?"

"I didn't think I'd still be here to know one way or another." She dumped sugar and cream into her coffee, took a quick swallow.

"You are, and I'm really curious about how a single mother living on a modest salary can afford to leave several thousand dollars in cash sitting on a table."

"I've always been good at saving money."

"Probably, but here's the thing, Merry. I've been sitting in my car, watching for your car since I left this afternoon. You never left the house, couldn't have gone to a bank. That means that you had thousands of dollars in cash just lying around your house."

"It wasn't lying around. It was hidden."

"Like your past? I told you I did some research while I was waiting. You got your first driver's license in your name four years ago."

"I lived in the city. I didn't need to drive."

He ignored that. "Here's what I want to know, Merry. If I were to subpoena your bank and get your bank records what would they show? A sudden influx of cash in the past week?" He shot out the question more to rattle her than anything else.

"What are you implying?" Her eyes blazed with fury, and he moved into her space, crowded her so that she couldn't run from the conversation. He could feel her harsh, uneven breath, sense the tension in her muscles.

"A woman is dead. You have more cash in your house than most people have in their savings account. Anyone can connect the dots and see what that means."

"What it means is that when I sold my parents' house, my siblings and I split the proceeds of the sale. I keep the money hidden in the house. It's my emergency fund. I have the paperwork from the sale if you need to see it."

"That might be a good idea."

"I'll dig it out in the morning. Hopefully, I can find it."

"Why do I have a feeling you won't?"

"I don't know, Douglas. Why don't you tell me what you think I've done, why you think I tried to run, why you think I have a pile of money in my house?" She dropped into a chair, her shoulders slumped, her face pale. She took a sip of coffee, the liquid sloshing onto the table and her hand. She didn't wipe it away, just stared down at the brown splotch.

"I think Tyler's father is after you. I think you're afraid of what will happen when he finds you."

The mug dropped from her hand, fell onto the table and broke, dark liquid rolling across the table and onto the floor. She jumped up, grabbed a handful of paper towels, and sopped up the coffee, her hands shaking so violently, he grabbed them, squeezed gently. "Who is he, Merry? Was he your husband?"

"No."

"A boyfriend then?"

"I don't want to talk about this!" She yanked away,

grabbed the trash can and swept the broken mug into it. Blood dripped onto the table, but she ignored it, grabbing more towels, wiping it up with the rest of the mess.

"You cut yourself." He lifted her hand, examined the cut at the base of her thumb, felt her pulse thrumming rapidly in her wrist.

He pressed a paper towel to the wound, and she pulled away. Turned away.

"Please, go."

"Did you see the guy who shot out your tires?"

"Not his face, but I think he was the same guy who was here the other night."

"Tyler's father?"

"No!" She nearly shouted, then took a deep breath. "Please, just go, Douglas. I've told you what I can."

"It's not enough."

"I'm sorry."

"Yeah, so am I. Because, I'm not going to let this go, Merry. I'm going to find out what's going on. With or without your cooperation. Set the alarm and lock the door. We'll have a patrol car outside your house for the rest of the night." He walked out of the kitchen, stalked to the front door, angry with her and with himself.

"Douglas." She put a hand on his arm before he walked out the door, looked up into his eyes. "If I were going to trust anyone, it would be you. I want you to know that. You're the only one who has ever made me think there was a chance to have…"

"Mommy!" Tyler called out, and Merry's hand dropped away.

"I need to go to him." And, she ran up the stairs, left him to lock the door from the inside, walk outside and walk away. From Merry and Tyler and the secret that haunted their lives.

He'd meant what he said.

He'd find out what he needed to know.

He just hoped he didn't destroy Merry's life in the process.

THIRTEEN

Fifty dollars to get the station wagon towed to the mechanic.

Four hundred dollars for three new tires.

A skull-splitting headache.

Victorian-era skirt and starched white blouse that itched and pulled and made Merry feel like she was suffocating.

Those things were not a good combination.

Especially not when she'd been afraid to bring Tyler to preschool. He rolled his toy fire truck up and down the aisle of the Reading Nook as she finished the second story hour of the day. Thank goodness Fiona had understood her need to have Tyler around. She had heard about the attack the previous night.

Of course she had.

More than half her family worked for the Fitzgerald Bay police department.

Merry ran a hand over her pulled-back hair to go with her costume, wishing she could loosen the heavy locks from the bun she'd fashioned that morning. The weight of it only added to her headache, made her stomach churn more. Made her want to sit down in a dark corner somewhere and cry.

Or maybe it was Douglas's words that made her want

to do that. His words, his actions, his compassionate blue eyes.

He was begging to be let into her life.

And she wanted to let him in so desperately she could feel it in every breath she took. Heaving out and in and pulsing through her. The need to confess it all, because he was going to find out anyway.

He would.

He already knew the name she'd grown up with. He just didn't know it belonged to her.

Lila Mary Kensington.

Mary to her family, because she'd shared her mother's first name. Now she had her mother's maiden name, as well.

Douglas would find out. Maybe, he already had.

But that wasn't the only reason she wanted to confess everything to him.

There were other reasons. Reasons that had more to do with the way she felt when he touched her hand, looked into her eyes, than with her fear that he'd find her out.

"Merry, are you okay?" Fiona touched her arm as the third-grade class Merry had been reading to dispersed.

"Just tired."

"You're pale as paper. Did you eat anything today?"

"I…"

"If it takes that long to answer, then you didn't. Why don't you take an early lunch break?"

"We have another group coming in a half hour. Fifth grade, and they're going to expect me to be here, dressed like a character in *Little Women*. I wouldn't want to disappoint them."

"A little disappointment won't hurt any of them, and I can handle the class." Fiona ran a hand over her auburn hair, then grabbed a cloth from her back pocket and dusted one of the tables that sat against one wall. Cozy reading areas were everywhere in the book store, and the Reading Nook had become as much a place to gather and talk as it was a place to purchase books. Merry had loved it from the moment she'd walked into the store. She still loved it. She just wasn't sure she'd be working there much longer.

The sick feeling in her stomach intensified as Fiona stopped dusting, looked straight into her eyes. "Douglas called me a few minutes ago."

"Did he?"

"He asked a lot of questions about you that I couldn't answer."

"If you want me to leave—"

"Why would I? You've been a good employee for a year. I trust you. I just wish you trusted me and my family."

"Fiona—"

The bell over the front door jingled, cutting off her words. Good. She didn't know what she would have said. What she *could* have said. She didn't trust anyone. Lately, she didn't even trust herself.

She turned to greet the customer, her smile tight, her head throbbing, Tyler's high-pitched imitation of a fire truck siren ringing in her ears.

"Please, Merry, tell your son to quiet down. Georgina is already fussy. The last thing I want is his incessant whine setting her off again." A tall blonde walked across the store, hair perfectly coiffed, trim figure encased in an immaculate pantsuit.

"Tyler, you need to quiet down. Ms. Christina—"

"I prefer that children call me by my last name. It just seems more proper and respectful," Christina Hennessy interrupted, and Merry bit back a sigh.

"Mrs. Hennessy wants you to quiet down, Tyler. Her baby might be scared by the noise."

"I'm sorry, Ms. Henny." Tyler looked up from his truck just long enough to offer an apology, then went back to his play.

"Hennessy," Christina huffed as she smoothed her hair, her diamond bracelet sliding along her too-thin wrist. Behind her, a nanny juggled one-year-old Georgina. Chubby-cheeked and adorable, Georgina gurgled and smiled as she watched Tyler push the fire truck.

"What can we do for you, Christina?" Fiona asked, and Christina frowned.

"I was wondering if the book I ordered is in."

"You have several on order, Christina. Which one are you asking about?" Fiona's tone was smooth and polite, but Merry sensed her tension. Like Merry, Fiona didn't much care for the spoiled wife of the town's premier lawyer.

"The child development book."

"The First Three Years?"

"Did I order another one about child development?"

"Not that I know of."

"Then that's the one. Is it in?" Christina snapped, and Fiona frowned.

"There's no need to be rude, Christina."

"Sorry. It's just been a long morning. The baby has been fussing since she woke up." Christina fingered her gold heart necklace and offered a brief smile.

"Maybe she's teething. Tyler fussed every time he cut a tooth," Merry offered, and Christina's gaze darted to Tyler.

"I'm sure he did."

"If Georgina *is* teething, a little teething gel will help with the pain," Merry continued, and Christina motioned for the nanny to bring over the baby. She lifted Georgina gingerly, frowning at the blond-haired, blue-eyed cherub.

"Do your gums hurt, darling?" she asked in a syrupy sweet voice that made Merry want to gag.

"I can run to the drugstore and get something for teething, Ms. Hennessey," the nanny offered, and Christina nodded.

"That's a good idea."

"Do you want me to take the baby?"

Christina hesitated, and then shook her head. "It's too cold to take her on a four-block walk, and it's too short a distance to drive. I'll keep her with me. We'll meet you at my husband's office when you're done."

"Yes, ma'am." The nanny hurried outside, and Georgina began to whimper.

"Hush. You're fine, darling." Christina bounced the baby on her hip, a tinge of impatience in her voice. "About the book, Fiona...*is* it in?"

"Not yet." Fiona typed something into the computer. "It *has* shipped, though. We should have it by Thursday."

"That seems like a long time to spend waiting for a book. I probably could have ordered it online and had it in by now."

"You're welcome to do that if you'd like."

"You're missing the point, Fio—"

The doorbell jingled again, and a blond-haired man walked in. Over a decade older than his wife, Burke Hennessy carried himself with authority, his sharp gaze jumping from woman to woman before it landed on his wife. "I thought you were coming to my office, Christina."

"We were on our way, but I wanted to stop in and pick up a book." She handed the baby to her husband, brushed invisible lint from her shoulder and arms.

"If we're going to go to lunch, we need to do it now. I have a meeting in a couple hours, and I need time to prepare for it. I explained that to you this morning."

"I remember. The nanny is picking up something for Georgina's teeth. I told her to meet us at your office." She pulled her coat sleeves down, adjusted the collar, and didn't seem at all intimidated by her husband's overbearing manner.

"Let's drive down to the pharmacy and pick her up, then. I really do have to get moving." He took his wife's arm and led her to the door, but stopped before he walked outside, his gaze bypassing Merry and settling on Fiona.

"Heard your grandfather was retiring from his mayoral position."

"That's right."

"I guess your father thinks he's a shoo-in for the job."

"We haven't discussed it." Fiona fiddled with the end of her hair, her green eyes flashing with irritation.

"I'm surprised. I thought the Fitzgerald clan discussed everything."

"We've been a little busy lately."

"Right. Unfortunately for your dad, he's not the only one who is considering running for office, and the people of Fitzgerald Bay might be happier to have a man like me in office than someone like him."

"Someone like him? What's that supposed to mean?"

"Everyone knows your brother Charles is responsible for Olivia's death, and we're all wondering why he hasn't been arrested. The way I see it, it all goes back to your father. He owns the police department. He arrests who he wants and allows people to go free when he wants."

"That's a lie!"

"Don't listen to him, Fiona. He's just trying to stir up trouble." Merry stepped between her boss and Burke, but there was no need. He'd said what he wanted, and he walked out the door without another word.

"I can't believe the nerve of that man!" Fiona muttered her body vibrating with anger.

"He's a blowhard. Everyone knows it."

"A blowhard who wants to cause trouble for my family." She took a deep breath, shook her head. "But it's okay. His accusations are groundless. My brothers, sister and father will prove that."

"Of course they will." At least, Merry hoped they would.

"I'm glad we agree. That makes me feel so much more confident." Fiona smiled, nudging Merry toward the door. "You go on ahead and take your lunch break, okay? I'm sure Tyler is getting hungry."

"Fiona—"

"I'm fine, okay? Just go have lunch and be back before the preschool class comes in. I can handle fifth graders but I'm not sure I'm up to corralling twenty-two little ones." Fiona smiled gently and grabbed Tyler's coat from a chair where he'd left it, handing it to Merry.

"All right." But Merry didn't want to eat. She didn't want to take a break. She wanted to do what she'd been trying to do the previous night—run.

"What are we going to eat, Mommy?" Tyler asked as she led him outside.

"I don't know. What do you want to eat?" she asked her gaze on the marked police car that sat across the street from the Reading Nook. It had been outside her house when she'd left for work, had followed her to her job. The officer waved, as she helped Tyler into the station wagon and she nodded in response.

An armed guard keeping her safe.

Merry wasn't sure if she should be thankful or frustrated.

She wanted safety, security, a feeling that she could ge

where she wanted, when she wanted, without having to look over her shoulder.

But she also wanted freedom to come and go as she pleased. No scrutiny. No silent police officer watching her every movement.

She finished buckling in Tyler, patted his hand. "Well? You didn't tell me what you want to eat?"

"Nothing."

"You're not hungry?"

"Nope. Just want to take a nap." He *did* look pale, his eyes shadowed from a restless night. Though he'd settled into bed quickly, he'd come to her room before dawn, climbed under the covers with her and cuddled close.

Bad dreams, he'd said.

Merry knew all about those.

She'd been having them for four years.

Had been living in one for all that time.

"Well, you have to eat something. You're a growing boy."

"But I'm not hungry, Mommy."

"I bet I know what would make you hungry."

"What?"

"Chicken fingers."

"We're going to Connolly's Catch?" The seafood store and restaurant served Tyler's favorite chicken fingers and fries, and he never turned down an opportunity to go there.

"Is there any other place to get chicken fingers?"

"No! Let's go!" He bounced in his seat, and Merry smiled. At least she could do *this* right. Bring him to his favorite restaurant, feed him his favorite food.

Not because it was the last meal they'd have together before her secret came out and she lost him.

No. She wouldn't even entertain that thought.

She'd bring him because they'd both been through a lot the past few days, and a little comfort food might be just the thing to get their minds off their troubles.

If only getting their minds off it could make it go away.

She glanced in the rearview mirror, saw that the police car had pulled onto the road behind her.

It kept pace behind her as she drove to Connolly's Catch and got out of the car. Cold wind speared through her coat as she grabbed Tyler's hand and led him across the parking lot and into the restaurant and seafood store. Warmth and the scent of fresh fish and homemade rolls enveloped Merry, and she slid out of her coat as she led Tyler to a small table in the corner. Fishnets draped from the ceiling and fishing rods crisscrossed the walls. Not a place she would have been interested in visiting when she lived in Boston, but she'd grown to love the casual atmosphere and the fun vibe of the place.

The fact that the owners spoiled Tyler only made it easier to visit.

"Is that my boy?" Vanessa Connolly hurried over, her freckled face wreathed in a smile.

"Ms. Vanessa! I'm going to have chicken."

"And fries, right?" Vanessa scribbled something on an order pad, and turned her attention to Merry. "Heard there was trouble last night. Are you both okay?"

"We're fine."

"Thank the good Lord for that. I'd hate to lose two of my favorite customers."

"All your customers are your favorite."

"But some have a special place in my heart. You want the Cobb salad?"

It was what Merry usually ordered but she'd had a long night, a long couple of days, and she wanted more than salad greens and boiled eggs.

"Actually, I'll have the fish of the day. We'll both have a small root beer." Another thing she never had and didn't allow Tyler to drink.

"Good choice, my dear. I'll have that for you in a few minutes. Don't want to keep you from work too long. Or, maybe you're not working and that Victorian getup you're wearing is all the new fashion rage."

"Even if it were the newest fashion trend, I wouldn't be wearing it unless I was working. It's tight and itchy."

Vanessa smiled. "I guess that explains why the Victorian misses look grumpy in their photos. I'll be right back."

She rushed away, and Merry settled into the chair, willing herself to relax, willing her headache away, willing herself to believe that things were going to be okay.

Beyond the parking lot, the bay stretched toward the horizon, choppy blue-green water lapping against the docks. Several boats were moored there. How much would it cost to rent one and hire a captain to sail her away?

A waitress set two small glasses of root beer on the table, and offered Tyler crayons and paper.

He scribbled happily, and the warmth of the restaurant, the easy flow of conversation and laughter seeped into Merry's chilled body, her eyes drooped, and she was tempted to close them, go ahead and let Vanessa cater to Tyler while she dozed.

"Here you are, Douglas," she heard Vanessa say. "The ladies will be very disappointed that you're not at tea, but I'm sure they'll get over it."

Douglas?

The name was like a splash of ice water in the face, and Merry straightened, her heart racing as she looked into deep blue eyes and a hard, handsome face.

Douglas.

"You don't mind sharing the table with my nephew, do you, Merry? The place is really hustling today." Vanessa didn't wait for an answer, just set a place mat and silverware at the end of the table and motioned for Douglas to pull over a chair.

He sat down, eyeing Merry solemnly as she shifted uncomfortably.

She wanted to get up, grab Tyler and run, but she knew he'd follow. "What are you doing here?" she asked, instead.

"I was supposed to come for tea this afternoon, but I decided to stop by a little early."

"Tea?"

"Vanessa invites me every couple months."

"I pictured you more as a coffee guy."

"You pictured right, but I love my aunt, and I can't say no to her invitations." His gaze dropped to Merry's high-collared cream-colored Victorian blouse, his lips curving into a half smile. "Cute outfit. I guess it was my sister's choice."

"Yes."

"You don't look happy about it."

"I'm not happy about anything today," she mumbled, and he covered her hand with his.

She wanted to pull away.

Wanted to hold on tight.

Wanted so much more than what was safe or reasonable or smart.

Her heart jumped at the thought, and she looked away, staring into the bay.

"You're not thinking of running again, are you?" His fingers smoothed over her knuckles, skimmed along her wrist, every touch trailing heat and reminding her of dreams she'd given up on long ago.

Romance.

Love.

Forever with someone who cared more about her needs than he did about his own.

She pulled away, rubbing her knuckles along her thick cotton skirt, trying to wipe away the heat of his touch, the longings of her heart.

"Not running. Just…getting into a boat and sailing into the sunset."

"Sorry to break the news to you, but that's not going to be possible."

"Because you won't let me leave town? I already know that. There's no need for a reminder."

"Because, the sun *rises* over the bay. It doesn't set there."

His words surprised a laugh out of her.

"In my dreams it *sets* over the bay, and I sail into it, okay?"

"What other dreams do you have, Merry?" His words flowed over her, smooth as melted chocolate, and she knew she could drown in them if she let herself.

Drown in him and all the things he represents.

Safety, normalcy, a place to settle in and become a part of.

He could give her that if she let him.

But letting him would mean giving up her secrets, and that would mean giving up the one thing she couldn't bear to let go of.

"I need to…use the restroom. Can you watch Tyler for a minute?" She didn't wait for him to respond, just ran, nearly knocking over the waitress in her hurry to put some distance between herself and the dreams she knew could never come true.

FOURTEEN

"That went well, huh, buddy?" Douglas asked, and Tyler looked up from the picture he was drawing, his eyes shadowed. Too shadowed for such a young kid.

"You going to watch me like my mommy said?"

"Yes. What are you drawing?"

"A picture."

"Looks like a two-headed dragon." Douglas eyed the colorful creature Tyler had drawn.

"It's a dog."

"With two heads?"

"He's got one head and two ears."

"Oh. I can see that." Sort of.

"Mommy says I can have a puppy in the spring." Tyler scribbled some more, the mark on his inner wrist peeking out a little more with every movement.

Douglas leaned close, trying to see it more clearly.

A scar of some sort, the skin raised and purple-blue. It looked like it had been caused by a deep burn, the edges sweeping in a curve that formed a perfect circle. Inside the circle, there seemed to be a shape of some sort. A triangle? A letter? Douglas ran his finger over the lines, traced what could have been an *R* or a *B*.

"What's this on your wrist, Tyler?"

"Nothing."

"Really? Then where did this mark come from?" Douglas touched the ridged flesh again. Definitely a burn. As a matter of fact, if he didn't know better, he'd think it was a brand.

The thought chilled him to the bone, and his hand dropped away, his stomach churning.

Had someone branded the little boy?

"Sorry about that." Merry returned to the table, her gaze dropping to Tyler's wrist, and then darting to Douglas.

"He has an interesting mark there. What's it from?" Douglas asked, and Merry's gaze dropped again.

"It's a scar."

"Right. *What's it from?*" He emphasized the question, willing her to tell the truth without him prodding and pushing and asking a million times.

"A burn," she hedged, not giving him everything, but not telling an outright lie, either.

"From?"

"It happened when he was a baby. I'm hoping it will fade more in time."

"You're avoiding the question."

She lifted her gaze, looked into his eyes.

Stark fear.

Deep longing.

He could see that she wanted to tell him everything, and he wanted to push her into it, force her hand by revealing the information he'd already learned.

But he wanted her to trust him, too.

Then, he could help her.

Then, they'd be a team with common knowledge and a common goal.

The waitress set plates in front of them, refilled their

drinks and walked away, and still, Merry held her silence and her secrets.

"Let's thank God for our food and eat, Ty. I don't want to be late getting back to work." She grabbed her son's hand, shifting his arm so that the scar was hidden.

"Can I pray, Mommy?" Tyler asked, reaching for Douglas, his chubby fingers soft and warm, his little hand swallowed by Douglas's. The idea that someone might have purposely scarred the kid made Douglas's blood boil.

He reached for Merry's hand, capturing it before she realized what he planned.

"You don't mind if I join your prayer, do you?"

"No. Of course not." But her hand was stiff beneath his, her words terse as she told Tyler that he could offer thanks for the meal.

She tugged away as soon as he finished, rubbed her fingers on her old-fashioned skirt, her hand trembling slightly.

"No need to wipe off my touch. I don't have cooties."

"I wasn't wiping away anything." She blushed and dug into her plate of fried fish.

"You're not very good at lying, Merry. I'm not sure why you keep doing it." It was a waste of their time. She must know that he'd learned the truth, or at least suspect that he had. He'd taken her fingerprints, after all. Told her flat out that he planned to run a background check. That had come up empty. Merry had no criminal record. Not even a parking ticket. What she did have was another name. He wanted to know why, and he wanted her to tell him.

"My mommy doesn't lie." Tyler frowned, his black eyes flashing with anger and what looked like tears.

"Hey, sport, I'm just playing around, okay?" He ruffled soft dark hair, his stomach clenching again as he looked into Tyler's face. A little boy shouldn't have circles beneath his eyes and fear in the depth of his gaze. He shouldn't have scars that looked like brands or danger stalking him.

"That's not a nice kind of playing around. I thought you were nice." Tyler's chin wobbled, a tear slipped down his cheek, and Douglas felt like the biggest loser on the planet.

"Don't cry, sweetie. Captain Fitzgerald was just kidding." Merry wiped away the tear, shot a heated look in Douglas's direction.

"What's going on over here? Why is my boy crying?" Vanessa appeared at the table, spearing Douglas with the same look Merry wore.

"That man said my mommy lies," Tyler wailed, and Vanessa lifted him from the chair, patted his back.

That man?

Douglas had thought they were buddies.

"How could you, Douglas? In front of the boy!" Vanessa hissed. "Of course, your mommy doesn't lie, dear one. Of course, she doesn't. Now, you just stop your tears. Dry them right up, because I have a cake that needs frosting, and I need you to help."

"Carrot cake?" Tyler sniffed back more tears.

"Isn't that your favorite kind?"

"It *is* my favorite!" Tyler sniffed again, and Vanessa smiled.

"Then, let's go frost it, and you can have a big piece when we're all done."

"Can I, Mommy?"

"You haven't eaten much of your lunch," Merry said, then sighed. "I guess you can finish when you come back. Go ahead."

"Thanks, Mommy!" Tyler wiggled out of Vanessa's arms, threw his arms around Merry, and for a fraction of a second, Douglas imagined moving in, scooping him up, tickling his belly. Apologizing again.

That man.

He'd come down a few notches in Tyler's eyes, and it bothered him more than he wanted to admit.

He waited until Vanessa and Tyler walked away, then turned to Merry. "I'm sorry about that. I should have thought before I spoke."

"It's okay." She picked at her food, not meeting his eye.

"No, it's not. Tyler is a little boy. He has nothing to do with your lies."

She dropped the fork, her face pale as she finally looked into his eyes. "You seem to have something you want to say. Why don't you just come out and say it, Douglas?"

"Because I'd rather *you* say it."

"I'm too tired for games. Just tell me what you want and we can both get on with our day."

"We found a match on the prints I pulled from a window sill at your place. They came up the same as some we pulled from Olivia's apartment. Want to guess who they belong to?"

"No."

"Then I'll tell you. They belong to a woman named Lila Kensington. A woman whose name you said you'd never heard."

"I said I'd never heard Olivia say it," she said, her voice weak.

"Can we stop playing games for a minute? Can *you* stop playing them? Just for a minute?" The anger that had burned in his gut since he'd learned the truth welled up and spilled out.

"I'm not playing anything," she choked out.

"Then why did your prints match the other two sets? Why does a background check reveal nothing about Merry O'Leary and plenty about Lila Mary Kensington?"

"I changed my name a few years ago. That's not a crime."

"Who are you running from, Merry?"

"Tyler's father." The words spilled out, and Douglas knew they were still only a partial truth.

"Why?"

"He's a dangerous man. I don't want him near Tyler."

"You're still hedging around the truth. You're still not telling me everything," he growled, and she winced.

"I—"

"Don't lie to me again, Merry. I need the entire truth if I'm going to help you and Tyler. *Everything*."

"I need to go. Fiona is expecting me back."

"Running won't fix things."

"Nothing can fix things." She tossed her napkin onto her plate, stood, but he couldn't let her go.

Not this time.

"We're not done talking, Merry." He didn't touch her, but she froze, her face so pale he thought she might pass out.

"I can't tell you anything more."

"You have to. Come on. We'll talk outside where it's more private."

"Tyler—"

"Is with Vanessa." He took her hand, led her onto the pier where his uncle docked his fishing boat. Led her to the very edge of the wood planking, so that the bay stretched out in front of them, the restaurant noise fading behind them.

She didn't protest, didn't speak as he turned her so he could look into her face. "It's time to stop running, Merry."

"I can't lose Tyler." Her voice broke, and a tear slipped down her cheek.

"Why would you?" He brushed the tear away, his palm resting on her cheek, some of his anger fading away as he looked into her face and read the terror and the sorrow there.

"Why?" he asked again, softly, quietly, because he didn't want to scare her more than she already was, didn't want to send her running again. She looked deep into his eyes for a split second before turning away, staring out into the bay.

Seconds ticked by, her silence stretching out as gulls cried and muted laughter drifted from the restaurant.

Finally, she spoke, the words so quiet he had to lean close to hear, and even then, he wasn't sure he had heard correctly. "He's not mine."

"*Who* is not yours?"

"Tyler. He's not my son. Not legally." Her voice broke and more tears slid down her cheeks.

"Then whose is he? Legally." He kept his voice steady, his tone gentle, but his pulse raced with shock. When he'd learned that she had run from Boston and changed her name, he'd assumed she'd been running from Tyler's father, that she was hiding her identity out of fear for herself and her son. He'd never imagined how deep her secrets ran.

"It's a long story."

"I have plenty of time to listen to it."

"Of course you do," she said, her hollow laughter drifting out into the bay, her face empty and cold, tears spilling down her cheeks. "Because, when you're done listening, you're going back to your home and your family and your life. But when I'm done telling it, my family won't be mine anymore."

"Why not? Whose son is he, Merry? If he's not yours, why are you raising him?" He captured her chin, forcing

er to look him in the eye. He wanted to see the truth when
he told it, wanted to know there were no more secrets be-
ween them.

"His mother was a student of mine. Her name was
Nicole Anderson. She was seventeen when we met. Eigh-
een when Tyler was born." The tears came more quickly
as she spoke, and endless stream of sorrow that made
Douglas want to pull her into his arms, hold her until
hey stopped.

"Where is she now?" he asked instead, because the
tory had to be told. All of it. No matter how painful.

"She's dead. Murdered a few weeks after Tyler was
born. Before she was killed, she asked me to take care of
Tyler until she could come for him. She was never able to
come, and I just raised him as my own." Her voice broke,
silent sobs wracking her body.

He tugged her into his arms, giving into what he wanted
and what he thought she needed. Holding her felt right,
comforting her felt right.

She felt right.

In his arms. In his life.

"I'm so sorry, Douglas. I just didn't know what to do."
Her head dropped to his chest, her hands clutching his
waist, tearstains splotching his leather bomber jacket.

"You didn't do anything you need to be sorry for. If
Nicole asked you to raise Tyler—"

"She did." She lifted her head, looked straight into his
eyes. For the first time since he'd met her, there were no
shadows in her gaze.

"Then you didn't commit a crime, and you have nothing to be afraid of. Not from the law, anyway. You said
you were running from Tyler's father?"

"Yes. His name is Tyrone Rodriguez. He's a high-
ranking member of the Boston Red Bloods, and I'm sure

he murdered Nicole. She told me he was capable of it. Told me he wanted his son and would do anything to get him.'"

Douglas knew the gang name. Notorious in Boston, they'd infiltrated many of Massachusetts's small towns and coastal villages, bringing drugs, illegal weapons and crime.

He thought of the mark on Tyler's arm. The circle with what could have been a letter in the center of it. He'd seen something similar on a gang member's arm. A new way of displaying the gang colors. A brand rather than a tattoo.

A brand!

"He branded his own son?" The question burst out, filled with every bit of Douglas's rage, and Merry jumped back, nearly tumbling off the edge of the pier. He grabbed her arm, holding her steady, his pulse racing with anger and fear. A man capable of branding his child was capable of killing without remorse.

"Yes. Two weeks after Tyler was born. Nicole brought him to me the next night. She was bloody and beaten and so scared for Tyler's life."

"Did you call the police?"

"She begged me not to. She thought Tyrone had connections in the Boston Police Department, and she was terrified that they'd take Tyler and give him back to his father."

"Tyrone Rodriguez is not a father. He's a monster," Douglas spat out, and Merry nodded, tears falling again, dripping down her face and dropping onto the wooden pier.

"Nicole had everything planned out. We'd both leave town. She'd go in one direction, and I'd go in the other. She'd lose Tyrone's tail, and I'd find a nice little town for her to settle in with the baby. She was going to call me once she knew it was safe. A week or two. That's all she asked of me, and I couldn't say no." Her voice broke, and she wiped away more tears.

"She never called?"

"I finally called her house. Her aunt told me that she'd been tortured and then murdered. It happened the night I left Boston. The next day, Tyrone visited Nicole's aunt, asked if she'd seen Nicole...or me."

"He knew your name?"

"Yes. He must have tortured the information out of Nicole."

"And then went to the aunt, pretending like he didn't know Nicole was dead?"

"That's what I thought when she told me about his visit. It's what I still think. Tyrone murdered Nicole, and I knew he'd kill me if he found me. Take Tyler. I couldn't let that happen, so I changed my name and I ran." Her tears had stopped, their tracks dried on her wind-whipped cheeks. Transparent, vulnerable, she was more beautiful than any woman Douglas had ever seen.

"You did the right thing." He slid a hand up her arm, let it rest on the back of her neck, the soft silky weight of her upswept hair heavy against his knuckles.

"Did I? I still wonder. I worry about what I'll tell Tyler when he's older. How I'll explain everything that happened, the decisions I made."

"Love, Merry. That's how you'll explain it. Come on. Let's go get Tyler. I want to bring him to the station while I make a few phone calls. Until we know where Rodriguez is, I want you and Tyler under twenty-four-hour guard." He walked toward the restaurant, but she grabbed his hand, pulled him to a stop.

"Douglas..." Her eyes glowed deep brown in her pale face, fresh tears shimmering on her long lashes.

"What?"

"Thank you." Her tears flowed again, down her cheeks, into his heart.

One minute they were apart, cold air and icy spray between them. The next, she was in his arms.

He didn't know how she'd gotten there.

Didn't care.

The feel of her, the scent, flowed over him and through him until all he knew was Merry. Her soft sigh, her eager response as his lips touched hers. Once. Then again.

Tentative.

Light.

Then, more and more, until he was lost in the moment. Lost in her.

Lost and hoping he'd never find his way back.

FIFTEEN

So, this *was what it was like to be swept off her feet.*

The thought flitted through Merry's mind.

There.

Gone.

Everything gone as heat flooded through her.

She moved closer to the source, wrapping her arms around Douglas's waist, her hands sliding up the firm, hard muscles of his back.

This was what it was like, and she wanted it to go on and on and on. Never wanted to let go of his strength and warmth.

"Hey! Mister! Why are you kissing my mommy?" Tyler's voice tugged her back to the cold winter day, the watery sunlight gleaming off the bay.

The terror.

She pulled back, gasping for breath as she looked into Douglas's vivid blue eyes.

"It's going to be okay. I promise," he said softly as Tyler raced toward them, Vanessa jogging along behind him.

Merry scooped Tyler into her arms, hugged him close. "I thought you were frosting a carrot cake."

"Already did. Why was he kissing you, Mommy?"

Tyler pressed his hand to Merry's cheek, demanding her attention.

"Now that's something for older folks to worry about, dear one. Not someone your age. Come on. We'll go back inside, and I'll sit with you while you eat your lunch." Vanessa's eyes gleamed with curiosity as she reached for Tyler, but Merry wouldn't release him.

She was too afraid of what might happen in the next days and weeks and months.

"Thanks, Aunt Vanessa, but can you pack it up for takeout? Merry and Tyler are coming back to the station with me. You want to see where I work, right, buddy?" Douglas asked, and Tyler's face brightened.

"We're going to jail! Yea!"

"I don't think I've ever heard anyone quite so enthusiastic about going to jail." Douglas laughed, ruffling Tyler's hair, the warmth in his eyes as he looked at her son filling Merry's heart.

She hadn't meant to tell him everything, but she'd wanted to so many times that when the words flowed out, they'd felt right and natural and good.

She'd trusted him with all the secrets she'd held close for four years.

She just hoped she wouldn't regret it.

Prayed she wouldn't.

She kissed Tyler's head, set him down when she wanted to hold him close.

What if Douglas couldn't help?

What if Family Services got involved and took Tyler away, gave him to Tyrone?

What then?

A piece of Merry would die.

That's what.

"He's going to be fine," Douglas whispered, his lips

brushing her ear, the contact shivering through her, reminding her that she wasn't alone in her struggles anymore.

But even that might not be enough to save her family.

The knowledge settled into her stomach, pounded along with the pain in her head.

"It's not nice to whisper. Right, Mommy?" Tyler bounced beside her, happy and sweet and loving, and she wanted to hold the moment close, tuck it away in her heart. Just in case.

"That's right, sweetie." She helped him into his car seat, her hands shaking as she tried to buckle him in.

"Let me." Douglas brushed her hands away, secured the straps, closed the door.

"Well, I had no idea you two were an item or I never would have invited you to tea today, Douglas," Vanessa said, walking over with their lunch in a bag and completely oblivious to Merry's fear and tension.

"We're no—"

"We didn't, either. Until a few minutes ago," Douglas responded easily, his gaze on Merry, his eyes so blue and filled with compassion they took her breath away.

"Well, I, for one, couldn't be more pleased. You two are a perfect match. If I've said it once to my dear husband, I've said it again. 'Douglas needs a woman like Merry O'Leary to settle him down.'"

"Let's not get ahead of ourselves, okay, Aunt Vanessa? Merry and I want to take our time and see where things lead. No pressure from you."

"Pressure? Since when would I ever put pressure on anyone?"

"Since all the time, but I love you anyway." He kissed her cheek. "We need to head out. Put lunch on my tab, okay?"

"Tab? What tab, you scoundrel? You're going to wash dishes next time you're in. Mark my words on that!" Vanessa laughed, Douglas winked and Merry should have felt so much better than she did.

So much stronger knowing she wasn't going to have to fight alone.

So much freer knowing that the truth had finally been told.

All she felt was sick dread.

Please, God, I can't lose Tyler.

"Everything really is going to be okay, Merry," Douglas said as he helped her into the station wagon.

"You can't know that."

"What I know is that you have a community of people who care about you. You have me. You have my family. You're not alone in this. Come on, let's get out of here. I'll follow you to the police department. No stopping for anything on the way there."

"Okay." She didn't want to stop. She wanted to drive and keep driving, but that would mean running again, and Douglas was right. It was time to stop. Time to face the past. Time to move on.

Knowing it didn't keep her hands from shaking as she drove to the police station, didn't stop them from trembling as she unbuckled Tyler and tried to keep him from darting across the parking lot ahead of her.

"Whoa, pal! Not so fast." Douglas lifted him onto his shoulders, Tyler squealed in delight and Merry's hands *still* shook. Her stomach shook. Her heart shook.

"What happens now?" she asked as they stepped into the police station.

"I'm going to take your statement, and then I'm going to contact the Boston P.D. I want to find out if they keep tabs on Tyrone. They may know if he's still in Boston."

"What about…?" She gestured to Tyler.

"We'll talk about that later."

"Right." That was for the best. She didn't want Tyler to hear the conversation.

"You two can sit in my office. I'm going to make a few phone calls from Owen's office."

Merry nodded, but she didn't want to wait.

Didn't want to sit in his office, thinking about the consequences of what she'd done. As much as she trusted Douglas, she wasn't sure she could trust the system. What if Tyler was taken from her? What if he was given to Tyrone?

She swallowed back panic, grabbing her cell phone and dialing Fiona's number. She had to let her know that she wouldn't be back in the afternoon, that she might not be back to work for a while.

"Reading Nook. How can I help you?"

"Fiona? It's Merry." Her voice was thick with tears and worry, and she cleared her throat.

"Is everything okay? You sound upset."

"I'm at the police station with Douglas."

"What's going on? You're not in any trouble, are you? If you are, I can close the shop and—"

"I'm not in trouble. I just…some things have come up. I can't explain everything right now, but I won't be able to return to work this afternoon."

"Merry, I'm worried about you. Last night, you were nearly killed. Today, you're at the police station. You know I'll help you in any way I can, right?"

"Yes, but I'm okay. I'm just waiting for Douglas to make a phone call, and then I'll be out of here."

"You're sure you don't want me to come?"

"I'm sure. I'll see you…" When? Until Tyrone was found, there was no way she could return to work. No way she could put Fiona's life in danger by leading Tyrone to her bookstore.

"Whenever you can come in will be fine. Call me when you can, okay?"

Merry said goodbye and rubbed her throbbing temples. Tyler sat at her feet, pretending to be a police car, his siren sounds piercing through her aching head.

"Can you quiet down, Ty? Mommy has a headache." She pulled pins from her hair, releasing the bun and taking some of the weight off the back of her head.

It didn't help.

The headache still pounded behind her eyes.

Tension and worry and fear pulsing a sickening rhythm through her blood.

Where was Douglas?

What was taking so long?

She glanced at the clock. Twenty minutes. Not so long after all. She tugged at the high collar of her Victorian shirt, wishing she could change into jeans and a T-shirt. Itchy, hot and grumpy, and still no sign of Douglas.

Where *was* he?

The door flew open, and she jumped up, nearly tripping over Tyler in her haste. But it wasn't Douglas in the doorway. It was his father. Haggard and windblown, his eyes shadowed and dark, Aiden smiled gently, and for a moment, Merry saw Douglas in his face.

"Everything okay in here?" he asked, and she knew Douglas must have asked him to check.

"I'm a police car," Tyler answered, zooming across the floor on his knees, his siren sound ringing in Merry's ears.

"A police car, huh? You like police cars a lot, don't you?" Aiden crouched down so he was eye to eye with Tyler.

"They're my favorite."

"Tell you what. How would you like to go for a ride in mine?"

"No!" Merry nearly shouted, everything she'd feared, everything she'd worried about suddenly coming true.

Aiden was going to take Tyler from her. Drive him to Family Services. Hand him over to a stranger.

"What's going on in here?" Douglas stepped into the room, looked straight into Merry's eyes, held her with his gaze.

Everything really will be okay.

She'd wanted so badly to believe him when he'd said that, but how could anything ever be okay again if she lost Tyler?

"You asked me to bring Tyler to my place until you and Merry are finished here, but she doesn't seem to want me to do it," Aiden responded.

"To your house? I thought…"

"I told you that you and Tyler were going to be under twenty-four-hour guard. The easiest way to do that is for you to stay at my father's place. Keira lives there, too. Between her and Dad and a top-notch security system, it will be very difficult for anyone to get to you."

"I—"

"If you'd rather me just bring the boy into my office for a few hours, I don't mind doing it, but I have toys for the grandkids at my place. Lots of toy police cars, too," Aiden offered, and Tyler's eyes widened.

"You do?"

"I do."

"Can I play with them?"

"Depends on what your mother wants," Aiden said, and he and Douglas both looked at Merry, waiting for her answer.

She couldn't refuse.

Tyler would be safe with Aiden, and it wasn't fair to make him sit around a police station when he could be playing. But it was so hard to let him walk away. "I guess you can."

"Yea!" Tyler threw his arms around her legs, and the hot tight feeling in her throat nearly choked her.

Don't cry.

Do. Not. Cry.

If she did, she'd upset Tyler.

"Come on, young man. Let's go take a ride in my police car." Aiden took Tyler's hand, led him from the room and it took everything in Merry not to run after them.

"My dad will take good care of him." Douglas hugged her, his hands stroking her back, his touch comforting and light. She could have stayed there forever. Let time pass and problems pass and pretend there was nothing to worry about.

Could have if it weren't for Tyler.

Her love for him outweighed everything else. Her concern had driven her farther than she'd ever believed she could go, pulling her from the siblings she loved, the home she loved, the city she loved. She'd learned how to obtain fake IDs. Learned how to pack light and drive fast. Learned what it meant to be completely and utterly alone.

Now, maybe, she needed to learn how to be part of a community again. Maybe, she needed to remember what it meant to be part of a team.

She stepped away, sniffing back tears as she dropped into the chair across from Douglas's. "What did you find out?"

"Nothing I was happy to hear." Douglas poured a cup of coffee, offered her one, but she declined, afraid she'd choke if she tried to swallow it.

"Tyrone isn't in jail, is he?"

"Not in jail, and he dropped off the radar a few days ago. Snitches inside the gang say he had some business to attend to."

"So he's here."

"Possibly. Take a look at this. Tell me if it's the guy who's been coming after you." He pushed a photo across the desk, and she lifted it. Dark hair slicked back from a broad forehead. Tan skin. Black eyes. Full lips twisted in a sneer. Handsome in a dark feral way.

A criminal.

A murderer.

Tyler's father.

But not the man she'd seen outside her house. Not the one who'd shot out her tires.

"It's not him."

"You're sure?"

"The guy I saw was blond, and his skin was much lighter."

"How about this guy, then?" Douglas handed her another photo, watching her intently as she studied it.

Blond hair. Blue eyes. Pale skin.

"It's him." She shuddered, handing the photo back.

"I thought so. I got a pretty good look at him last night. Two years ago, Tyrone took over as gang leader. The blond is his second in command. Kent Don. He dropped off the radar around the same time as Tyrone."

"So Tyrone *does* know Tyler and I are here."

"They know Lila is here. They don't necessarily know you're Lila. They were probably staking your place out, trying to figure out whether or not you're the person they've been looking for. There's something else. Boston P.D. said there were rumors after Nicole's death. People on the street said she took something valuable from Rodriguez, and he wanted it back. That might have been the motivation for her murder. Unfortunately, rumors aren't enough to convict someone of a crime."

"Do you think Tyler was what he valued and wanted back?" She couldn't imagine the man who'd murdered Nicole finding value in any life.

"Maybe, but I'm wondering if there was something else. Last night, Kent could have easily killed you. There's no doubt he's a good shot. Three bullets. Three tires shot out. If he'd wanted to hit you, he could have, but he didn't aim for you. I've been wondering why not."

"I don't have anyth—" But she did.

She had money. She had the journal.

"You've thought of something." Douglas leaned forward, the excitement in his eyes unmistakable.

"Nicole left a diaper bag with me. I was so scared, I took it and my purse and ran. A couple of hours later, I stopped to feed Tyler and I found twenty-thousand dollars and a journal in the bag."

Douglas whistled softly. "That's a lot of money."

"I thought Nicole must have stolen it from Rodriguez, but I couldn't go to the police with it. I was too afraid Rodriguez would hear about it and find me."

"What about the journal? Was there anything in it?"

"Notes to Tyler. Thoughts about Nicole's pregnancy and about her hopes for Tyler's future." Merry had read it only once. Nicole's emotions were so powerful, so beautifully written that she'd cried for hours afterward.

"You still have the journal and the money?"

"Yes. The money is in a bank account, accruing interest. The journal is back at my place."

"I'd like to have some people look through it, see if there's anything you missed. Once they're finished, you'll get it back. We'd better head over there now. There's a nor'easter blowing in, and I want you at my dad's place before then."

"What about you?"

"I have work to do."

"But the roads might—"

"Remember what my aunt said about us being an item?" He tugged her to her feet, and her breath caught as she looked in his eyes.

"Yes."

"I like the idea of it."

"Of us being an item?" Her heart skipped a beat as he trailed a finger across her lower lip.

"Of us being a perfect match. There's just something about you. There has been since the day I saw you in my sister's store. I can't ignore it, can't turn away from it. So don't worry about me working during a nor'easter. I have too many things I want to find out to let a storm ruin things for me."

"What things?"

"Things like what you'll look like without fear in your eyes. Like what it will feel like to walk in the moonlight with you by my side. To taste the laughter on your lips." He bent so that they were a breath apart, and her heart raced with longing for all those things.

"Douglas—"

The door opened, and Ryan Fitzgerald walked in, his gaze jumping from Merry to Douglas. "Sorry. If I'd realized I'd be interrupting something, I would have knocked."

"You should have knocked, anyway. What's up?" Douglas hooked an arm around Merry's waist, his fingers playing along her side, and she didn't have the strength to move away.

"I have news about that toxicology report we were waiting on. It came out clear, and I need to speak with you. Alone. Sorry, Merry, but it's business."

"It's okay." She blushed, tried to move, but Douglas didn't release his hold.

"Stay here, okay? No breaking for the border."

"I'm done running," she said and meant it even more when he smiled.

"Glad to hear it. I'll be back in a few minutes." He walked into the hall with Ryan, leaving the door open so she could see the hallway, hear voices, feel the presence of others.

She needed that.

Despite everything Douglas had said, despite his reassurance, she was afraid.

Of Tyrone.

Of Family Services.

Of Douglas and what she felt when she was with him.

She'd dreamed of those things years ago. Of butterflies in her stomach. Of sweet kisses and moonlit walks. She'd dreamed of marriage and kids and family, and then she'd given up on those dreams. Shoved them away, because she hadn't believed they'd come true.

But maybe they could.

Maybe they would.

Maybe God had brought her to Fitzgerald Bay so that she could face her past, walk into her future.

And maybe Douglas was part of what that future would be.

She was almost afraid to think that, almost afraid to hope for it.

She'd been struggling for so long. She'd been alone with Tyler for so long. What would it be like to have someone in her life? Someone in their lives?

Someone Tyler could look up to.

Someone she could trust with all her secrets and her dreams.

She wanted that.

And she was beginning to think that maybe, just maybe, God wanted it for her, too.

SIXTEEN

"You're getting a little chummy with our star witness aren't you, bro?" Ryan asked as they walked into the small conference room at the end of the hall.

"I guess I am."

"You think that's a good idea?"

"I don't think it's a bad one. Merry told us what she knows. She's given us a key piece of evidence. Any relationship with her isn't going to impact the case one way or another."

"So you're in a relationship?" Ryan raised a dark eyebrow, gave Douglas the look he'd been giving him since they were in grade school. The one that said, *I'm your big brother, and I know a lot more about life than you do.*

"Jealous?"

"Hardly." Ryan laughed. "Women are too much work. I prefer to put my time and effort into other things."

"That's what you're saying today. Tomorrow, the perfect woman might walk into your life."

"And I'll tell her to walk right back out. I've got no desire to settle down."

"We'll see how that works out for you," Douglas responded.

Ryan smiled.

"Back to business. Olivia's cousin, Meghan Henry, called again. She's talked to a few of Olivia's friends in Ireland. No one there seems to know about a boyfriend. As I mentioned, I also heard from the medical examiner. The toxicology report came back clean, but we did get a match on the blood found on the rock. The medical examiner confirmed it's Olivia's."

"We thought there were two blood types on the rock. Was that confirmed, too?" That was a piece of information they were keeping close to the cuff. No sense in letting a killer know he'd left behind forensic evidence.

"Yes. We had blood typing come back on both of them."

"And?" Douglas had been praying the blood on the rock wouldn't match Charles's blood type, but the look in Ryan's eyes told him the bad news before his brother spoke it. "It's the same as Charles's, isn't it?"

"I'm afraid so."

"And you think that's good news?"

"I think it is. We're going to run DNA tests. I've already called Charles in to give a sample. If DNA can be extracted from the blood on the rock, we'll be able to prove to the gossip mongers that he wasn't the killer."

"Good, because I've already had a few people imply that we should have done more than bring Charles in for questioning."

"They've probably been talking to Burke Hennessy."

"What does Hennessy have to do with it?" Douglas asked, though he was pretty certain he knew the answer. A well-known lawyer, he'd served on the town board and had a reputation for having an arrogant disregard for the opinions of others.

"He was in the Reading Nook earlier. Fiona said that he heard that Granddad is retiring and asked her about it."

"And?"

"He wants to be mayor."

"Let him run. He's had verbal altercations with half the town. I doubt any of those people will vote for him. Dad has nothing to worry about."

"That's not what concerns me. Hennessy told Fiona that the murder investigation isn't being handled properly because Dad wants to protect Charles. If you're hearing grumbles, I'd lay odds that Hennessy is behind them."

"*He's* talking about a conflict of interest? That's ridiculous. There's no evidence pointing to Charles. No motive." Douglas paced across the conference room, looked out over the parking lot. He loved the community, but small towns bred big gossip, and it seemed the Fitzgeralds were currently caught in the middle of that.

"He didn't use those words, but that's exactly what he's saying. It's not something we aren't aware of, so it's not a surprise that others are noting it." Ryan rubbed the back of his neck and sighed. "Look, I've got a ton of paperwork to do, and I'm already looking at a late night. How about we talk about this more at our next meeting?"

"When will that be?"

"As soon as I clear my desk enough to schedule one. Probably the end of the week."

"Sounds good." But Douglas couldn't quite shake his frustration as he left the conference room.

His father had served Fitzgerald Bay for decades. The family had served the community for longer than that. They'd always conducted their work with integrity and honor. They were reared to do so. The idea of the residents whispering and speculating was like a dagger to the heart.

"You look upset," Merry said as he walked into his office.

"Politics. They get to me every time." He didn't tell her

everything. She had enough troubles without adding his into the mix.

"You don't seem like the kind of guy who lets things like politics bother him."

True. He wasn't, but this was about family. It was about loyalty. It was about all the things that he'd been taught to value.

"Usually, I'm not."

"Then why are you this time?" She stood and stretched, her hair falling nearly to her waist as she leaned back, and his stomach tightened, his senses jumping to life. He wanted to bury his face in her hair, forget the gossip and politics and trouble.

"How about we talk about it later?"

"Why? Because it's okay for me share my troubles with you, but it's not okay for you to share yours with me?" She frowned, her dark eyes flashing.

"That has nothing to do with it."

"Of course it does. I've told you my deepest secrets, but you won't even tell me why you walked in the room looking like you wanted to take someone's head off."

"You have enough to worry about, Merry. You don't need to worry about my problems, too."

"What I don't need is for you to treat me like some delicate hothouse flower. I can handle trouble. I've been handling it for four years." She stalked out of the room, her irritation obvious in every step.

He followed her into the parking lot, waiting until they were close to her car before he pulled her up short.

She swung around, mouth tight, obviously ready for a fight.

But he didn't want to fight.

He wanted her, and he wouldn't hide that. Not from his family. Not from himself. Certainly not from Merry.

"If you were a flower, you'd be a winter rose, and if I were a little smarter, I'd have told you what you wanted to know when you asked."

"I…" she started to say. Frowned. "You don't play fair, Douglas."

"What would fair be?"

"You refusing to admit that you were wrong so that I could stew and grow resentful and find a reason to…"

"What?" He twirled a red-gold curl around his finger, let it go, watching as it sprang back into place.

"Forget my dreams again."

"Dreams, huh? Do they include me?"

"They might. If you stop trying to protect me from everything," she said, and he smiled, knowing that he'd been right when he'd said they were a perfect match. Not perfect people. Just better together than they would ever be apart.

"In that case, maybe I do need to start sharing my troubles with you, because I really like the idea of being part of your dreams." He took car keys from her hand, opened the door to the station wagon.

"Then tell me. What's got you so upset?"

"Not what. Who. Burke Hennessy."

"He was in the Reading Nook this morning."

"I heard. I also heard he's been spreading the same trash talk all over town."

"He's an arrogant jerk, and everyone knows it."

"People tend to forget who the good guys are and who the bad guys are when they're in the middle of a gossip fest."

"You're worried about Charles, aren't you?"

"Among other things. There's talk that the department isn't handling the investigation properly, and that we should be digging deeper into Charles's life and motives."

"You're doing your job, Douglas, and you're doing it well. Anyone who knows your family, knows that."

"Like I said, people tend to forget."

"*I* won't. Now we'd better get going before my son tears your father's house apart." She started the engine, and he nodded.

"I'll follow you to your place. Don't get out of the car unless I'm there." He closed the door, jogged to his SUV, worry for Charles, for Merry and for Tyler churning in his stomach.

The quiet town he'd grown up in was suddenly filled with drama and trouble. First, Olivia's murder. Then the attacks against Merry. Now the gossip that seemed to be spreading like wildfire.

Nothing that had been found at the scene or in the apartment that indicated Charles's presence at the time of Olivia's murder. Not a hair. Not a footprint. Not a fingerprint. None of that would matter if people got word of the matching blood type.

Douglas needed the DNA tests to come back quickly, and he needed them to be conclusive. It was the only way to clear Charles in the town's eyes and to clear the department of any supposed wrongdoing.

It was the only way to stop the gossip and Burke Hennessy.

He frowned as he pulled into Merry's driveway, saw her getting out of her car.

"I thought I told you to stay in your vehicle until I was here," he said as he grabbed her arm, surveyed the area, shielding her from the street as he led her up the porch steps. No sign of trouble, but that didn't mean it wasn't there.

"You *are* here," she countered, and he frowned again.

"Next time, wait until I'm out of my car. We don't know if Tyrone or Kent Don are hanging around waiting for an opportunity to put a bullet through your skull."

"Nice image, Douglas." She unlocked her front door, and stepped into the foyer, froze.

"What's wrong?" He stepped in behind her, saw the chair in the living room turned over, stuffing spilling from the slashed cushions. Sofa pillows lay on the floor, their insides exploding onto the ground. Books torn from the small shelf in the corner, their covers strewn across the floor.

Chaos.

Everywhere.

Adrenaline pumped through him as he surveyed the damage, his senses alive, every cell in his body straining for some sign that he and Merry weren't alone.

"Stay behind me," he ordered, but Merry broke away, racing up the stairs as if there wasn't every possibility that the perp was still hanging around just waiting for her to return.

SEVENTEEN

Tyrone and Kent had broken in.

They'd ransacked the house.

Had they found the journal? It was the only hard evidence Merry had that the story she'd told was true, and she'd need it when she petitioned for custody of Tyler. It had to still be here.

She raced up the stairs, ignoring Douglas's shouted command as she skidded into her bedroom. Torn curtains, shredded books, ripped up mattress, dresser drawers tossed on the floor, their contents scattered about. Everything exactly like it had been in the living room. Completely destroyed.

The closet door yawned open, its contents dumped on the floor. She ran to it, her heart thundering in her ears as she yanked up the floorboard.

Money.

Bankbook.

Journal.

Everything just where she'd left it.

Thank You, Lord.

She shoved the journal into her purse, reached for the bankbook and cash, tossing them in with it.

"Are you nuts? Someone could still be in here." Doug las dragged her to her feet.

"I was afraid that they got the journal. Without it, I can prove that Nicole wanted me to raise Tyler."

"Would that have mattered if you were dead?" he hissed, anger flashing in his eyes.

"I—" Hadn't thought about that, but she should have Should have remembered that Tyrone had killed th mother of his child and that he wouldn't hesitate to kil her once he had what he was after.

A floorboard creaked in the hall. Stealthy footstep padded on hardwood.

Tyrone moving in to do what he'd probably been plan ning for four years?

She froze, staring into Douglas's eyes, hoping he wasn going to die because of her.

Hoping *she* wasn't going to die.

He pulled a gun, his movements so smooth and quie she barely realized what he'd done. Only knew for sur when she saw the weapon in his hand.

"Get in the closet and stay there," he mouthed, nudg ing her back and closing the door, the soft click soundin like a firecracker.

She stood in the tiny area, heart racing, the hair on th back of her neck standing on end.

Silence.

Darkness.

Everything still.

And, then it wasn't.

A crash and a muffled shout. Another crash, and some thing slammed into the closet door with enough force t crack the wood.

Then finally she heard Douglas's voice—he was call ing for backup.

She shoved open the door, raced into the room, her feet tangling in discarded clothes. She pitched forward, hands out, as she slammed into a hard chest.

"I told you to stay in there," Douglas growled, as he pocketed his phone. Taut muscles moved beneath her hands, and she was so thankful he was okay, so relieved he was alive, that she threw herself into his arms. "This is my job, Merry. It's what I'm trained to do. *You* are trained to teach kids. The next time we're in a situation like this, and I tell you to stay put, stay put!"

"Next time? You think there's going to be a next time?" she responded, her gaze on the person lying a few feet away.

Hands cuffed behind his back.

Blond hair. Gaunt features. Eyes closed. She knew him, had seen him outside her house, seen him in her rearview mirror, would probably be seeing him in her nightmares.

"It's Kent Don."

"And his boss might not be far behind."

"You think Tyrone is here, too?" Just the thought made her skin crawl.

"I don't know, and you're making it difficult to find out."

"I'm not—" Sirens cut her off, and Douglas held up a hand, silencing her as footsteps pounded on the porch stairs and an officer announced his presence.

"We're upstairs. One perp in custody. Another may be in the house," Douglas called out, and Merry tensed.

Was Tyrone hiding somewhere in the house?

Sounds carried from downstairs, voices, footfalls, doors opening and closing. Someone walked up the stairs. More doors opened and closed.

"All clear, Captain." An officer stepped into the room. Not someone Merry knew, and he didn't pay her any attention as he dragged Kent to his feet and read him his Miranda rights.

"Get your hands off me, cop! I want a lawyer," Kent growled.

"You'll get one, but first, I want to know where your boss is." Douglas stepped toward him, his expression cold and hard.

"I don't know what you're talking about." Kent smiled, and the hair on the back of Merry's neck stood on end. Evil. That's how he looked, and she moved closer to Douglas.

"Maybe I can jog your memory. Tyrone Rodriguez sent you here to find Lila Kensington. Where is he?"

"He didn't send me here for nothing. I came to fish." Kent smiled again, and Merry shuddered.

"Where is he?" Douglas stepped into Kent's space, taller, broader, tougher than the young thug, and Kent's smile fell away.

"He's in Boston. Now, back off before I start screaming police brutality."

"He hasn't touched you," the officer responded.

"I may if he doesn't start talking," Douglas muttered. "Take him down to the station, book him and get him a lawyer. I'll be there to interview him as soon as I finish here."

"Will do." The officer dragged Kent from the room, and Douglas turned to Merry, his eyes blazing.

"Don't ever do that again. You could have been killed running up the stairs the way you did."

"I don't plan on it. As a matter of fact, I may just stay locked in your father's house for the rest of my life." Her voice shook, and he sighed, tugging her into his arms.

"You still have the journal?"

"In my purse."

"Kent disconnected your alarm system, and then tore this place apart looking for something, and I have a feeling the journal might be it. Can I take a look?"

"Sure." She pulled it from her purse and handed it to him.

"I've only read through it once, but there's nothing in it. Just Nicole's thoughts about her pregnancy and Tyler." He studied the cover, ran his fingers over the letters and numbers carved into the leather.

"What's this?"

"I don't know. Nicole carved it, though. She mentioned it in a letter she wrote to Tyler."

"Yeah? Where's that?"

"Inside the back cover."

It took several seconds for Douglas to finish reading. Finally, he looked up. "She really loved him."

"Yeah. She did." Merry blinked back tears, and Douglas closed the journal.

"In the letter she says that Tyler will find his father's name hidden on the cover of the book. Have you found Tyrone's name on it?"

"The letters are there, but there are other letters, too, and I've never taken the time to try to figure out what they all mean or how they're connected. Nicole always loved codes. She wanted to be a cryptologist, and I think she would have been a great one."

"We'll send a copy of the cover and the letter to an expert. See what he can figure out."

He led her outside as the first flakes of snow began to fall, and she pulled her coat close as he helped her into the SUV, waited while he rounded the vehicle and got in.

"Are we going to your father's place?"

"*You* are, and I want you to stay there."

"Where else would I go?"

"I don't know, Merry, but until Tyrone is apprehended, you can't afford to take needless risks. Stay at my father's place. Do what he tells you. I'll be back to update you as soon as I can."

"What's going to happen after this is over?" she asked as he pulled away from the house.

"Hopefully, Tyrone and Kent are going to go to jail for a very long time."

"I mean, with me. With Tyler."

"You're going to live happily ever after. Isn't that the way these things always work out?" He glanced her way, a half smile turning up the corners of his lips.

"Not always."

"This time it will. Eventually, you'll have to go to court to petition for legal custody of Tyler. For now, you'll clean up your house, you'll go back to work. Everything will be almost exactly the way it was."

"Almost?"

"Tyrone will be out of your life. The threat he presented will be gone. You'll be safe. And, *I'll* be *in* your life."

"Douglas—"

"If you're going to tell me it won't work out, don't. We can't know until we try, and this time we *are* going to try. No secrets between us. No lies. Just us trying to see if what we feel when we're together is as real as it seems." He pulled up in front of a large colonial-style house and turned to face her.

"I wasn't going to tell you it wouldn't work out. I was going to tell you how thankful I am that you're in my life and that you're planning to stay in it."

"Then I guess my lecture was for nothing." He smiled, pressed a quick kiss to her lips, the brief contact searing into her. "Are you going to be okay here for the night?"

"Yes."

"We'll talk more tomorrow, okay?"

"Thank you. For everything."

"I don't need your thanks. I just need you. Safe. Happy. Here in Fitzgerald's Bay."

"I—"

"Hey! Douglas! Stop talking and get moving. We've got a suspect to question." Keira Fitzgerald, rookie officer, rapped on the glass and peered into the driver's-side window.

"We?" Douglas got out of the car, and Merry did the same.

"Dad says it will be a good experience for me."

"Will he say the same if I ask him?"

"He'll say that I talked him into letting me be there, but he still agreed to let me come along. Sorry you've had so much trouble, Merry. Hopefully, we can get things cleared up for you."

"We *will* get things cleared up, but let's get Merry settled in first."

The front door opened and Tyler raced out, a toy police car in each hand. "Mommy! Look what Mr. Chief gave me!"

"They're wonderful!" She lifted him, ignoring his squirming as she held him close and inhaled deeply. Shampoo and soap and little boy all mixed with a hint of chocolate. "Have you been eating chocolate before dinner, young man?"

"Mr. Chief said we should always eat dessert first."

"Funny, he never said that when I was growing up." Douglas ruffled Tyler's hair.

"That's because *you* never taught me how to bounce like a ball," Aiden responded as they walked into the foyer.

Douglas laughed, and Tyler wiggled down, skipping

into a beautiful living room, his smile so broad Merry was sure his cheeks must hurt.

This was what Merry had craved for so long.

Connection.

She hadn't just craved it for herself. She'd wanted it for Tyler. He deserved this. Deserved to be caught up and pulled in and made to feel like he belonged. Not for a few weeks or months or even a year. Forever.

"Look, Mommy! More cars." Tyler tugged her to a lineup of cars, and she sat down next to him.

Douglas joined them, his gaze on Merry. "You're going to stay here, right?"

"I told you I would. I'll be here when you get back."

"Then I'd better go, so I *can* get back." His lips brushed hers, the contact so light she felt it in her soul more than on lips.

And then he was gone, tossing a quick goodbye at his father as he headed out into the falling snow.

EIGHTEEN

Tyler slept fitfully, his little face scrunched up in a scowl that tore at Merry's heart. After all the happiness of the afternoon and evening, he seemed to be having nightmares, and she rubbed his head, murmuring softly when he groaned in his sleep.

She glanced at the clock.

Nearly midnight.

She should be sleeping, too, facing her own dreams and nightmares.

Instead, she paced the large guest room, the howling wind pressing against the windows and making the old house creak in protest.

It had been hours since Douglas and Keira left. Hours since Aiden had led Merry and Tyler to the guest room. Hours spent thinking about what might happen. *Worrying* about what might happen.

Despite Douglas's reassurances, she couldn't help being scared. Tyler deserved so much more than a gangster father. He deserved to be cared for and loved and made to feel safe.

That's what she had been giving him for four years.

What if she went to court, petitioned for custody and was denied?

If Tyler was taken away from her, would he remember her in a year or two? When he was a teenager, would he wonder what had become of the first mother he could remember?

She shoved the thought away.

Dwelling on what could happen wouldn't change anything. She just had to trust that God had already made the decision, and that He'd chosen Merry to be Tyler's mother.

"Merry?" Aiden called out, tapping softly on the door, and she hurried to open it, her heart racing. "There's been a bad accident on the highway outside of town."

"Is Douglas okay?"

"He's fine. He wasn't involved in the accident, but it's a fifteen-car pileup. The State is coming in to help, but it's our jurisdiction, and we need all hands on deck. I have to head out there. Will you be okay here by yourself?"

"Tyler and I have spent four years by ourselves. We'll be fine. I just hope that everyone involved is okay."

"It sounds like we've got multiple injuries. I'm praying none of them are serious, but the sooner I get there to help direct traffic, the less likely it will be that more cars will be involved and more people hurt. I'll set the alarm before I leave. The doors and windows are locked. Keep them that way." He had the same blue eyes as Douglas, but they didn't shine with warmth and humor. Instead, they were serious and just a little sad.

"I will."

"On a night like tonight, I can't imagine Rodriguez trying to get you, but if you have any trouble, call the station directly. The 9-1-1 lines are tied up with calls about the accident, and I don't want you to have to wait for rescue if Rodriguez does show up. You have the number?"

"I have Douglas's number." She pulled her cell phone from her purse and shoved it into the pocket of her robe.

"Don't be afraid to use it. He's still at the station, and he should be able to get here quickly despite the road conditions."

"I'll call if I need him." But she hoped she wouldn't. Hoped that Kent had been telling the truth when he'd said Rodriguez was still in Boston.

"Not just if you need him, Merry. If you even suspect that you might need him. A strange sound, a bad feeling, anything that makes you think Rodriguez could be lurking around, you call. Understand?"

"Yes."

"Good girl." He patted her shoulder, offering a reassuring smile before he hurried away.

Merry stepped back into the room, smoothed Tyler's hair, and then paced to the window, watching as Aiden pulled out of the driveway, his emergency lights flashing, his sirens blaring.

Gone.

And she was alone.

Alone.

She'd told Aiden that she was used to it, but she couldn't say she liked it. Not tonight, anyway. Not with the wind howling and the house creaking and Rodriguez stalking her.

Maybe tea would help. Aiden had told her to help herself to anything in the kitchen, and she walked down the stairs, rubbing her arms against a chill she couldn't quite shake.

Outside the storm raged, snow flying against the windows as gusts of wind carved ditches and created drifts. One of the biggest snowstorms of the century. That's what the meteorologists were saying, and Merry believed it. Several inches of snow already covered the road, and the trees bowed under the weight of the heavy flakes.

She shivered, her hand resting on the cell phone as she boiled water for tea and turned on the television. News of the accident filled every station, and Merry prayed for the victims as she watched images of the scene flash across the screen.

A bad night to be out.

Surely, Tyrone wouldn't be.

She tried to reassure herself, as she settled onto the living room chair and listened to news reports about the weather and the accident.

He *wouldn't* be.

She sipped tea, wind howling outside the window.

Wouldn't be.

No way.

Something scraped against the living room window, and she jumped, her heart racing as she slowly turned to look.

Nothing.

No face leering in at her from the darkness. No eyes glittering from behind the glass.

Her cell phone rang, and she grabbed it, desperate to talk to someone. Anyone.

"Hello."

"You took something from me. I want it back." The voice seemed to slide into the room, fill the space, steal Merry's breath.

"Who is this?"

"You know who it is. You know what I want. You want the kid, have him. But I want what's mine."

"I don't know what you're talking about."

"My girl gave it to you."

"The money? You can have it. I haven't spent—"

"Not the money. The other thing she gave you. You give it back to me. I let you live. You keep playing games keep pretending you don't know what you've got, and you die. Tonight. And the boy? He just might die, too." He disconnected, the dial tone ringing in Merry's ear for several seconds before she realized he'd hung up.

How had he gotten her number?

She pictured her trashed house, papers and bills strewn everywhere. He'd been in her house before she and Douglas arrived. Found the number on an old bill.

Called her.

From where?

Boston?

Her place?

Right outside the window?

Fear clawed its way up her throat, stealing her voice as she called Douglas.

"Hello?" His deep baritone filled her ear, and she forced words past the terror.

"It's Merry."

"Good. I was about to call you. Dad said he got called out to an accident, and I want to—"

"He called me. Tyrone Rodriguez. He called. He said I have something of his, and he wants it back."

"Are you sure it was him?"

"He didn't give me a name, but he said I could keep the kid, and he said that his girl gave me whatever he thinks I have. It has to be—"

"Stay put. Do *not* open the door for anyone. I'll be there in ten minutes."

"I—"

But he was gone, and she shoved the phone back into her pocket, turned off the television and the living room light. Listened to the howling wind, the creaking house, her erratic heartbeat.

She needed to find a weapon. Something that she could defend herself and Tyler with if Tyrone showed up.

Most of the Fitzgeralds were police officers. There must be a gun in the house somewhere.

Only she wasn't sure how to use a gun. Didn't know how to load one. Wasn't sure she could fire one even if she managed to get it loaded.

No. A gun was out. She needed something that didn't need instructions and training and a few years of target practice.

She ran into the kitchen, searched the drawers until she found a steak knife, her hand shaking as she lifted it.

Please, God, don't let me have to use this.

Something banged against the back door, and Merry jumped, her pulse racing, adrenaline pumping, every nightmare she'd ever had about to come true.

Let it be the wind, Lord. Please, just the wind.

She crept to the door, pressed her head against the wood, heard nothing but her pulse slushing in her ears and the endless howling of the wind.

A minute passed, and she was sure she'd been mistaken. Sure that there was nothing outside but a raging winter storm.

Please, just let it be the storm.

Bang!

The door vibrated with the force of the blow, and she fell back, the knife dropping from her hand.

Stupid. Stupid, stupid, stupid.

Don't drop the knife just as he comes crashing through the door.

She scrambled to retrieve it, sliding across the floor on her knees, grabbing the knife as the lights went out and the room plunged into darkness.

Was Tyrone trying to turn off the alarm?

Had he succeeded?

It didn't matter.

Nothing mattered but protecting Tyler.

She backed away from the door, her heart thudding painfully, the wind howling, the house rattling, the nightmare standing right outside the door.

Please, God, get Douglas here quickly.

Crash!

The door flew open, snow flying in Merry's face, the shrieking alarm covering the sound of her terrified scream.

A shadow moved through the doorway, darkness hiding his face, but she knew who he was, couldn't stop her body from shaking in response.

She lifted the knife as he lunged toward her, tried to plunge it down, to stop him before he made it to the stairs and Tyler, but he grabbed her wrist, twisted so brutally, the knife dropped from her numb fingers.

She screamed in pain, in fear, and he twisted harder, shoving her into the wall.

"Where is it?" he shouted in her ear, his hot breath making her skin crawl.

"I don't know what you're talking about."

"Liar." He slammed her into the wall again, and she felt herself slipping away.

Tyler.

His name anchored her to consciousness, and she smashed down on Tyrone's foot, tried to break free of his brutal grip.

"Stop fighting and give me what I want. Either that or die." He pressed something cold to her head.

Something hard.

A gun!

He had a gun.

He'd use it. She knew he would. Even if she hadn't known he'd killed before, she would have been able to hear the intention in his icy tone, feel it in his taut muscles.

I'll be there in ten minutes.

Douglas's words filtered through the terror.

Ten minutes.

At least four had passed.

Six more minutes and help would arrive.

She just had to stay alive until then.

She threw herself backward, slammed her foot down on Tyrone's instep again. He cursed, shoving her away with so much force she bounced off the wall, her head hitting the corner of a cabinet.

She fell hard, her injured wrist snapping as it took the full force of her weight.

She saw stars, knew she couldn't hold on to consciousness.

But somewhere, Tyler screamed, his terrified cries barely audible beneath the high-pitched screech of the alarm.

She had to get to him.

Had to protect him.

"I said give me my stuff!" Tyrone dragged her to her feet, his face so close she could see it through the darkness, smell the stale tobacco on his breath.

"I don't have anything of yours."

"You do. And you got one more minute to hand it over. You don't, and you die. And after I'm done with you, I'm going to take care of the kid."

"He's your son!"

"And hers. The witch stole from me. You think I can allow that?" He shook her, slamming her into the wall so violently the breath left her lungs.

"I—"

"Shut up! We don't have time to talk. Show me where you put the book."

"What book?"

He backhanded her, and she saw stars, tasted blood.

"You think this is a game, lady? I've spent four years looking for you. Went through a lot of trouble to track you down. A lot of trouble. Nikki said she gave you the journal and the directions to my stuff are in it. I figure what a woman says when she's got a gun pressed to her head is the truth. So, tell me. Where's the book?" He pressed the cold barrel of the gun to her temple.

Stall him.

Tell him something that will keep him from pulling the trigger.

Once you're dead, there will be no one to protect Tyler.

Tell him something.

Tell him.

"It's in my purse." The words tripped off her tongue, thick and heavy with fear.

"Where is it?"

"Uh...in the living room." She couldn't bring him upstairs. Couldn't lead him to her screaming son.

"Let's go." He shoved her, and she fell, sliding across the floor, her right hand and arm useless.

"Get. Up!" He grabbed her hair, yanked her to her feet, dragged her out of the kitchen and down the hall.

"My Mommy! Where are you, My Mommy?" Tyler shrieked from the top of the stairs.

My Mommy.

Tyler's code words for *I'm scared. Come and get me.*

But she couldn't go to him. Couldn't take him in her arms and whisper in his ear and tell him that everything was going to be okay. Couldn't smooth his thick hair, wipe tears from his cheeks. Couldn't. And that hurt more than her throbbing wrist or her aching head. Hurt worse than any physical pain ever could.

Her son needed her.

She couldn't help him.

All she could do was lead Tyrone past the staircase and into the living room, Tyler's frantic cries stabbing holes in her heart.

If she died, he would die. If she died, all the things she'd wanted for him would cease to matter. She'd never know how it all would have turned out. What kind of man Tyler would have grown into. What kind of mother she would have become as years turned into decades.

If she died, she'd leave her life just when it seemed like she could start living it again. Just when she'd started to believe that there'd be a happy ending to the story that had begun the day Nicole walked into her classroom in Boston.

If she died all the things she'd seen in Douglas's eyes, all the dreams she'd begun to dream again…they'd die with her.

So, she wouldn't die.

It was as simple as that.

She would not die.

She wrapped the thought up tight in her heart as she walked through the living room and pretended to search for her purse.

NINETEEN

"Slow down, Douglas. You're going to get us both killed. Then what will happen to Merry and Tyler?" Keira's voice penetrated the fog of Douglas's terror, and he eased up on the gas.

She was right.

Conditions were terrible, the nor'easter howling its fury as it blew snow across icy pavement.

But he didn't want to slow down. Didn't want to spend even one extra minute trying to get to his father's house safely. His brother Owen had called a few minutes ago to report that the alarm system at their father's house had been triggered.

Which meant Tyrone had gotten in.

"Dear God, please don't let him hurt Merry and her son," Keira prayed out loud, and Douglas stepped on the gas again.

Stepped down hard, taking the turn onto his father's street a little too quickly. The SUV slid, and he righted it, turning off his headlights as he drew closer to the house.

No sense letting Tyrone know they were coming or giving him a reason to kill Merry quickly.

If he hasn't already killed her.

He shoved the thought aside.

Refused to entertain it.

God had brought Merry into his life for a reason.

He didn't believe it was so that he could watch her die.

He wouldn't believe it.

The house was dark. Not a light on inside, and Douglas parked a few houses down. Turned off the engine, hopped out of the SUV.

"You're not going to run in there without a plan." Keira grabbed his arm, jerked him to a stop.

"I have a plan. Find Rodriguez and stop him."

"I may be a rookie, but I know that's not the kind of plan we need. If he's in there, if Merry and Tyler are still alive—"

"They are," he said with more venom than he intended.

"Then we can't risk running in there without some idea of what we're going to find and how we're going to react."

"I can tell you exactly how I'm going to react. I'm going to stop him. Just like I said." But she was right. Running in without a plan was foolhardy. "Okay. Here's what I want to do. I'll go around back. You search the front. Look for his point of entry. We need to move in quiet and slow. If we spook him, he might kill Merry or Tyler."

"And if I find the point of entry?"

He wanted to tell her to wait for him. Wanted to tell her to back off and let him handle it. She was his baby sister. The little girl he'd loved to tease, and who'd always laughed at his jokes.

But she was also a cop.

A rookie, but a crack shot.

She could handle herself, and he had to let her do it.

"Go in. Be careful, though. It's dark, the alarm is screaming, we don't want to shoot the wrong person." He left her with that, racing around the side of the house, the

vind hiding the sound of his feet as he probed the darkness, tried to find Tyrone's point of entry.

There!

The back door hung open, banging into the wall again
and again. He stepped inside the kitchen, the screaming
alarm piercing his eardrums.

Go slow.

Take your time.

Don't get yourself killed.

Don't get Merry or Tyler killed.

Beneath the sound of the shrieking alarm, the muted
cries of a child echoed rhythmically.

My Mommy. Mommy. My Mommy.

Over and over again.

Tyler's cries, but no answer from Merry.

The thought of what that might mean speared his heart,
twisted his gut.

Please, God, don't let me be too late.

Douglas prayed frantically as he eased into the hallway,
his gun out and ready. He made sure the foyer was clear.
Walked toward the front door.

A gunshot exploded, and a woman screamed, the sound
barely carrying above the alarm.

Douglas knew the voice. Heard the terror.

Merry.

Alive.

He ran into the living room, not caring about flying
bullets. Not caring about anything but finding Merry.

Shadows writhed on the floor. Two people locked in a
death roll. Too dark to see. Too risky to shoot.

"Police! Freeze!"

He tucked his gun back in its holster, dove into the
chaos, grappling with Merry's assailant.

Strong. Wiry.

"Die, cop." Rodriguez shifted, and Douglas grabbe his wrist, feeling rather than seeing the gun he held.

"I don't think so." He slammed Rodriguez's hand int the floor. Once. Twice. The gun clattered on hardwoo and slid away.

Douglas grabbed it, pressed it to Rodriguez's temple.

"*Now* are you going to freeze?" he panted, and Rodr guez went still.

The alarm cut off, the silence so abrupt, Douglas's ea buzzed with it.

A light illuminated the hall and splashed into the livin room, but Douglas didn't look to see who'd turned it o Didn't dare turn his attention away from Tyrone until h was sure the gang leader was under his control.

He wanted to slam his fist into the snarling face c Merry's attacker but flipped him over instead, patting hi down. "Do you have any other weapons on you?"

"I want a lawyer."

"You'll get one. Do you have any weapons?"

"Figure it out yourself, cop," Tyrone spat, and Doug las slapped handcuffs on his wrists, read him his Mirand rights, then turned his attention to Merry.

She lay a few feet away, her wrist bent at an unnatu ral angle, her face deathly pale, blood seeping throug her hair. He touched her neck, desperate to feel her puls speeding beneath warm skin.

"I called for an ambulance. Is she okay?" Keira race into the room, skidding to a stop near Rodriquez.

"I don't know." Despite her son's still-frantic cries, sh hadn't moved, hadn't opened her eyes. "Merry?"

Keira tugged Rodriguez to his feet, shoved him out tł door, and Merry stirred, mumbled Tyler's name.

"He's okay."

"I need to get him." She brushed his hands away, stoo

swaying, shaking, blood dripping down her head onto her shoulder.

No. Not onto her shoulder. From her shoulder onto the floor.

"You've been shot. You need to sit down before you fall down." He put an arm around her waist, tried to lower her to the ground, but she shook her head.

"I'm okay. The bullet just grazed me."

"And your wrist is broken. Your head is bleeding."

"And my son is calling for me, and I'm not going to lie on the floor while he screams himself sick." She took a step, her legs going out from under her, and Douglas lifted her, carried her from the living room into the hall, set her down on the bottom step.

"Moooooooommmmmmy!" Tyler screamed from the landing, the anguish in his voice tugging at Douglas's heart.

"It's okay, buddy. Everything is okay," Douglas repeated as he climbed the steps toward Tyler.

He lifted the little boy, wiped tears from his face.

"Mommy. My Mommy. Where's my mommy?" he sobbed, and Douglas carried him down the stairs, set him in Merry's lap, then dropped down on the step behind her, supporting her back as she pulled Tyler close.

He felt the moment like nothing he'd ever felt before.

Felt Merry's tension ease, Tyler's muscles relax, felt them meld into each other, knew he was melding with them, becoming part of their circle of affection, connection, love.

"Thanks for running to my rescue. Again," Merry said, shifting so she could look into his face.

"Again? We're not keeping tabs, are we?" He brushed curls from her cheek, and she smiled.

"*I* am."

"Don't, because I'd do it a million times to keep you and Tyler safe."

"Let's hope you don't have to." She rested her head against his shoulder, and his heart leaped in acknowledgment.

This was how it should be. Merry in his arms. Tyler in his arms. Safer together than apart. Happier together than apart.

Better together than apart.

He didn't release his hold as EMTs filled the room, crouched over Merry and Tyler and him.

"Ma'am, you're going to have to let us take your son." An EMT tried to ease Tyler from Merry's arms, but she opened her eyes, shook her head.

"No. We're going to the hospital together, or I'm not going."

"You have some serious injuries, and holding on to your son is only going to make them worse."

"A broken wrist isn't serious."

"Your head—"

"I'll take Tyler," Douglas assured her. "We'll meet you at the hospital." He eased around, put his hand on Tyler's back.

"You're going to drive him to the hospital in the middle of a snowstorm?" Merry frowned.

"Why not?"

"The roads are terrible. You could get into an accident."

"I'll drive slowly."

"But—"

"Don't worry, Merry. I have no intention of letting anything happen to any of us." He lifted Tyler from her arms, patting the little boy's back, that feeling he'd had coming back. The melding and meshing and claiming.

This *was* how it should be.

For sure.

Forever.

"I already know that something is going to happen," Merry said as the EMT helped her onto the gurney.

"Yeah?"

"The way I see it, we're going to do exactly what you said we would."

Her eyes drifted closed, and he touched her cheek to assure himself that she was still warm and vibrant and alive.

"What's that?" he asked, and she smiled, her eyes still closed.

"Don't you remember, Douglas?" she responded as the EMT started wheeling her away. "We'll live happily ever after."

TWENTY

"Ouch!" Merry muttered as Dr. Charles Fitzgerald put another stitch in her shoulder.

"You're feeling pain?" He looked up from his work, his blue eyes so much like Douglas's that Merry blinked.

"No, but it looks like I should be."

"So don't look." He offered a half smile, his brown hair falling over his forehead.

"I have to. It's like watching a train wreck. I'm horrified, but I can't look away." And she wished she could, because her stomach wasn't feeling all that hot.

"Then I guess it's a good thing I'm almost done. Last stitch." He finished quickly, bandaged the wound and stood to wash his hands. "That should do it. You'll stay here for observation tonight. Tomorrow, you can go home, but you'll have to be careful. That son of yours is a live wire. I don't want him tearing out all my hard work."

"I'll be careful."

"Listen." He turned, the harsh overhead light casting dark shadows beneath his eyes. He looked exhausted, his skin paler than she'd ever seen it. "I heard about the situation with Tyler. I want you to know that you have my full support. You're a great mother, and I'd be happy to testify to that in court."

"Thank you, Charles. That means a lot to me."

"Yeah, well, it means a lot to me that you didn't run screaming from the room when I walked in." He smiled, but there was no humor in his eyes.

"Why would I?"

"Some people think I had something to do with Olivia's death."

"How could anyone think that? You're one of the kindest men I know," she responded truthfully. She'd always liked Charles's calm bedside manner and the easy way he interacted with Tyler. "Tyler loves you. Fitzgerald Bay loves you. Really, what other doctor would come out on a night like this to work triage at the local hospital?"

"A major accident means lots of patients, and the hospital needs all the help it can get. It's not really a statement of my character that I'm here."

"I think it is."

"That's because you have a good heart, Merry, and you're a good person. Like I said, I'll be happy to testify on your behalf when the time comes."

"And I'll be happy to tell anyone who cares to listen that you did not murder Olivia."

"Words won't help me, I'm afraid. I need proof, and that seems to be hard to come by. I have to check on a couple patients. Try to rest. The stitches will need to come out in ten days. I want you to have a follow-up X-ray on the broken arm in forty-eight hours. If things are healing nicely, you won't need surgery. If they're not, I'll give you a referral to an orthopedic surgeon." He walked out of the room before she could reply.

It was for the best.

She didn't know what to say.

Had no words that would ease the sting he must feel

knowing that people who he cared about and had cared for were turning their backs on him.

"You're frowning." Douglas stepped into the room, Tyler asleep on his shoulder, and Merry's heart leaped.

Happily ever after.

When she looked at Douglas and Tyler together, she really could believe in it.

"I was just thinking about how unfair it is that your brother has served as the community physician, helping people when they need him but when *he* needs *them,* they turn their backs on him."

"Not many of them."

"Would it matter if it were only one? It still must hurt."

"It does, but my brother is tough. He'll get through this."

"Have you been able to find any evidence that will clear him?"

"Charles isn't a suspect to anyone but a few overly imaginative people. There's no reason to try to find evidence to clear him of something he didn't do."

"But you're trying, anyway, aren't you? Trying to find something that will keep the rumors from spreading and keep your brother from being hurt more than he already has been. *Have* you found anything?"

"I'll admit, we're looking, but it's an open investigation and I'm not at liberty to say what we've found or haven't found."

"Meaning that you haven't found anything yet, right?"

"I guess you don't understand what 'I'm not at liberty to say' means." He smiled, pulling over a chair near the bed and sitting in it.

"*I* understand. I was just hoping *you* didn't."

"I'd share with you if I could, but there are rules, and

have to follow them. Now, if you want to talk about *your* case…that we can discuss."

"I guess that might be interesting, too. Are Tyrone and Kent talking?"

"They've both lawyered up, but it doesn't matter. We have Kent on breaking-and-entering charges, and we have Tyrone on attempted murder."

Attempted and almost successful murder.

If Douglas and Keira had been even a minute later…

Merry shuddered, pushing away the thought.

"Maybe my case isn't that interesting after all." She didn't want to dwell on what could have been. Didn't want to think about Tyrone or Kent. She'd rather rejoice in what was.

"Then how about we change the subject to something I find much more fascinating." Douglas's gaze dropped to her lips, and she blushed.

"What's that?"

"Happily-ever-afters." He ran his hand down her arm until they were palm to palm, warm flesh to warm flesh.

"What about them?" she breathed, her voice wispy and light, her breath gone as he smiled into her eyes.

"Every good love story has one."

"Is that what we are?"

"What do you think, Merry?" He shifted Tyler, leaning down to capture her lips. Tenderness, warmth, love, they flooded out of him, flooded into her, and she wanted to drown in them. In him.

He broke away, his breath uneven, his eyes dark as he smoothed hair from her face. *"Are* we a good love story?"

"You know what? I think we are."

"Think?"

"If the judge agrees to grant me legal custody of Tyler,

I'm going to be a package deal. Not every man would be happy about that."

"There's no *maybe* about it. You'll be granted legal custody. Which means it's a really good thing that I'm not every man and that I've always been partial to package deals." He lifted her hand, gently kissed her knuckles, and she felt love building, felt forever building.

"Have you?"

"Of course. There's nothing better than finding one thing you love and figuring out something else you love comes with it."

"Do you always know the right thing to say?"

"If you ask me, yes. If you ask anyone in my family, the answer might be different."

She laughed, her eyes closing of their own volition, her thoughts drifting.

"You know I'm a package deal, too, right?" Douglas's lips brushed her ear, his words so soft they almost seemed part of the dream world she was falling into.

"You have children?" She frowned, forcing herself to pay attention, to wake up enough to figure out what he was saying.

"No."

"A dog or cat?

"I'm afraid not."

"Then what comes in the package?"

"A very big, very exuberant family."

A family?

The *Fitzgerald* family?

She pictured them all. Stately Ian. Steady, hardworking Aiden. Ryan, Owen and Keira, dressed in their uniforms. Charles with his stethoscope and tired eyes. Fiona with her auburn hair and quirky bookstore ideas.

A package deal?

She figured it was a good one.

After all, the Fitzgeralds were pillars of the community. Hardworking and honorable. Loyal and tight-knit. More than that, they loved without reservation, they served without thought to their own needs. They valued faith and family, and that was clear in everything they did, everything they said.

They were a wonderful group of people.

And Douglas, he was the most wonderful of all.

She looked into his face, looked into his eyes, felt all those things she thought she never would. Felt all her dreams springing to life again.

"You know what, Douglas? I think that's going to end up being the package deal of a lifetime," she said, and then she hooked her uninjured arm around his neck and pulled him down for another kiss.

EPILOGUE

Fitzgerald Bay Courthouse

Silent as a tomb, the courtroom seemed to hold its breath as it waited for the judge to arrive.

Or, maybe, it was just Merry who held her breath.

Her throat clogged, and she forced back tears. She'd cried so much during the past three weeks beginning with Olivia's death, she didn't know how she could have any tears left.

"Breathe, Merry, or you'll end up on the floor, and Jethro Shaffer will take a picture and post it on the front page of the *Fitzgerald Bay Gazette*," Keira hissed, patting Merry's back with a little too much force.

"I can't believe you're worried about such a thing on a day like today," Vanessa Connolly said, and Keira shrugged.

"I can't, either. But it really burns my boat that we've had to allow this trial to be made public just to prove that we're not manipulating evidence or people." She scowled, shooting daggers at Burke and Christina Hennessy.

"It's okay that it's public," Merry said.

"It is not okay. It isn't okay by a long shot."

"Shhhhh. Do you want to get us kicked out?" Fiona whispered, and Keira fell silent.

Merry glanced at her watch for what felt like the fiftieth time, wondering why the minute hand didn't seem to be moving. Two minutes and the judge would arrive. Two minutes and she'd know what the future would be.

"Can I take your seat, Keira?" A familiar voice washed over her, and Merry stood, threw herself into Douglas's arms.

"I thought you were stuck in Boston." He'd traveled there to view the evidence the Boston police had found when they decoded the message on Nicole's journal. It had revealed the address of a bank where Nicole had opened an account in Tyler's name. A safety deposit box there contained a piece of paper that listed Tyrone's drug contacts in Mexico and the dates of his drug transactions. With that in hand, the police were putting together enough evidence to try him for Nicole's murder.

"There was no way I was going to miss this." Douglas had dark circles under his eyes and stubble on his jaw, but nothing could distract from his gorgeous smile.

"I'm glad you're here. Your sisters are about done with my nerves."

"I'm sure you haven't been that bad—"

"All rise!" the bailiff called, and Merry squeezed Douglas's hand, her eyes on Tyler. He sat just a few feet away, his feet swinging under his seat as he sucked on a lollipop Aiden had given him.

"It's going be okay." Douglas held her hand as the judge walked into the room, and she wanted to believe he was right.

"I see we have a full courthouse again today. I can't say I'm pleased," the judge said as she took a seat. "Bailiff, if you could take the minor into my chambers, I have a special treat for him there."

The bailiff took Tyler's hand and led him from the courtroom, and Merry's heart constricted, her body numb with fear.

"I won't beat around the bush with this, since I know everyone is anxious. Counsel, approach the bench. Ms. O'Leary, you may approach the bench, as well."

She wanted to.

She really did, but her legs were like Jell-O, and she wasn't sure they would hold her.

Douglas squeezed her hand, and she looked into his eyes, saw his confidence, his certainty.

"Go," he mouthed, and she went, approaching the bench, looking into the judge's eyes.

"Breathe."

Merry wasn't sure if she was hearing Keira or her oxygen-starved brain's desperate plea, but she inhaled, exhaled. Heard the judge speaking through the whooshing of blood in her ears.

"I've heard from the counselors. I've heard from witnesses. In the end, though, what matters most to me is not the testimony of character witnesses or psychologists or doctors. What matters most is the child himself. There is obviously a very strong bond between the minor and Ms. O'Leary, but that is not enough."

Merry's heart dropped, the tears she'd been holding back began sliding down her cheeks.

"Children must be fed an abundant diet of love and attention. They must understand their value and worth. More than that, children must always know they have a loving and safe place to go home to. Tyler has found that in you, Ms. O'Leary. That, combined with the evidence submitted by your counsel and the testimony of the witnesses, has led me to grant your request. You are hereby awarded legal custody of Tyler Rodriguez. Congratulations. Court is adjourned."

The courtroom erupted in applause and cheers, but Merry barely heard.

She was too busy running toward Tyler as he was led out of the judge's chambers, an oversize teddy bear in his hands.

"Mommy!" He giggled as she lifted him, hugged him tight.

"We did it!" Douglas pulled them into his arms, wrapping them in an embrace as warm and welcome as a summer day.

She burrowed in, Tyler wiggling and giggling as he was sandwiched between them.

"I know." She sniffed, but the tears just kept pouring down her face.

"Then why are you crying?" He brushed moisture from her cheeks, his touch tender and light and filled with love.

"Because, happily-ever-after wouldn't have been so happy without all of us in it."

"There was never any worry that would happen." He smiled, but something in his eyes made her heart catch.

"What's wrong?" she asked, letting go of Tyler, letting him run to Aiden's side.

"Nothing that you need to worry about."

"We're not going back to that again, are we?" she asked, and he raised an eyebrow.

"What?"

"That thing where you treat me like I'm going to break."

"You *did* break. As a matter of fact," he said, lifting her casted arm, "you're still broken."

"And healing nicely, according to your brother. So, tell me what's wrong."

"We've got a new guy joining the police force."

"When did that happen?"

"I just heard the news. He'll be starting this week. It's good. We need the extra manpower. I'm just worried that Burke will start planting thoughts in the new guy's head. Get him digging around and looking for trouble."

"He's not a local?"

"No." Douglas sighed, ran a hand through his hair.

"That doesn't mean he's going to buy into Burke's conspiracy theories."

"It doesn't mean he won't, either."

"It's going to be okay, Douglas." She squeezed his hand, and he smiled.

"Isn't that my line?"

"It used to be, but I thought I'd try it on for size, because I really do think everything is going to be okay. Once the DNA evidence comes in, Charles will be completely cleared in the eyes of the community. Soon, you'll find Olivia's murderer. I know you will. The new guy will probably even help you do it."

"I'm glad you have so much confidence."

"Why wouldn't I? You and your family are a pretty impressive team." She patted his cheek, and he captured her hand, looked into her eyes.

"You're pretty impressive, too. So how about we stop talking about the murder investigation for today? This is a time to celebrate, and I know just the way to do it."

"Dinner out?"

"With Tyler? I don't think so, Mer. I love the kid, but he can't sit still long enough to eat a chicken nugget let alone a four-course meal." He wound his fingers through hers, took a step closer.

"Then, what do you suggest?"

"Something that begins like this." He tugged her in, kissed her with a passion that left her breathless.

"Go on." She slid her arms around his neck, inhaling his masculine scent, not caring that Jethro Shaffer was standing ten feet away, just waiting to snap a picture.

"And ends like this." He kissed her again, and she was sure lightning flashed.

Or maybe it was Jethro's camera.

She didn't know, didn't care, as she looked into Douglas's warm blue eyes.

"So, what do you think?" he asked, his voice just a little uneven, and she smiled.

"I think I really like the beginning and the end. What comes in middle?"

"How about we work that out together as we go along?" He grabbed her hand, tugged her toward Tyler, toward his family and toward all the dreams they'd build together.

* * * * *

Dear Reader,

When I was a kid, summer and winter vacations meant trips to Massachusetts to visit family. Since then, I've had a love for New England. Beautiful fall foliage, cold crisp winter, bright blue summer sky… You can't beat it for seasonal changes, nor can you help feeling the history of the places you visit there. It thrilled me to be asked to participate in a continuity series set in the area. The small town of Fitzgerald Bay is quaint and tight-knit, the people that live there full of character and strength. Writing the story of Douglas Fitzgerald and Merry O'Leary brought me back to those wonderful days I spent with people I loved in a place I loved. It also reminded me of God's power. Even in the worst times of our lives, even when we aren't sure we've made right decisions, done the right thing… even when we know we haven't… He is there, His love so powerful and strong, His desire for us so great that it rises above our failures and pulls us back to Him again and again.

I hope that you enjoy the first book in the Fitzgerald Bay continuity series.

I love to connect with readers. You can visit me at http://shirlee-mccoy.blogspot.com, connect with me on Facebook or drop me a line at Shirlee@shirleemccoy.com

Blessings!

Shirlee McCoy

Questions for Discussion

1. Four years ago, Merry O'Leary made a decision that changed her life. Would you have made the same one? Explain.

2. When she arrived in Fitzgerald Bay, Merry felt an affinity for the small town and the people there. What other reasons did she have for staying?

3. How did the burden of Merry's secrets impact her relationship with the townspeople?

4. How did it impact her relationship with Douglas?

5. Why do you think she agreed to go out to lunch with him?

6. Douglas has a reputation for being the town's most eligible bachelor. How does he feel about that?

7. When he sees Merry for the first time, what is it that catches his attention? What is it that keeps it?

8. Merry has made two promises. One to Olivia. One to Nicole. How do those promises influence her decisions after Olivia's body is discovered?

9. A lie is a lie, and the Bible is very specific about God's feelings regarding lying tongues. Merry felt forced into lying because of her fear for Tyler. Explain your feelings about this. Was there a way she could have protected her son and told the truth?

10. Olivia's murder is the catalyst that forces Merry to allow Douglas into her life. She is reluctant but unable to refuse him. Have you ever had a time in your life when something you haven't wanted has been thrust onto you? How did the experience change you?

11. At what point do you think Merry begins to truly trust Douglas? Does it happen before or after he finds out the truth?

12. Faith and family is the Fitzgerald family motto. How does Douglas show that he lives by this?

13. Do you think that Merry regretted her decision to flee Boston? What makes you think this?

14. In Merry's circumstances, what would you have done?

15. Who do you think killed Olivia?

INSPIRATIONAL

Wholesome romances that touch the heart and soul.

Love Inspired®
SUSPENSE

COMING NEXT MONTH
AVAILABLE FEBRUARY 14, 2012

DANGEROUS IMPOSTOR
Falsely Accused
Virginia Smith

THE ROOKIE'S ASSIGNMENT
Fitzgerald Bay
Valerie Hansen

PROTECTING THE PRINCESS
Reclaiming the Crown
Rachelle McCalla

SHATTERED IDENTITY
Sandra Robbins

REQUEST YOUR FREE BOOKS!

2 FREE RIVETING INSPIRATIONAL NOVELS
PLUS 2 FREE MYSTERY GIFTS

Love Inspired
SUSPENSE

YES! Please send me 2 FREE Love Inspired® Suspense novels and my 2 FREE mystery gifts (gifts are worth about $10). After receiving them, if I don't wish to receive any more books, I can return the shipping statement marked "cancel". If I don't cancel, I will receive 4 brand-new novels every month and be billed just $4.49 per book in the U.S. or $4.99 per book in Canada. That's a saving of at least 22% off the cover price. It's quite a bargain! Shipping and handling is just 50¢ per book in the U.S. and 75¢ per book in Canada.* I understand that accepting the 2 free books and gifts places me under no obligation to buy anything. I can always return a shipment and cancel at any time. Even if I never buy another book, the two free books and gifts are mine to keep forever.

123/323 IDN FEHR

Name _____ (PLEASE PRINT)

Address _____ Apt. #

City _____ State/Prov. _____ Zip/Postal Code

Signature (if under 18, a parent or guardian must sign)

Mail to the **Reader Service:**
IN U.S.A.: P.O. Box 1867, Buffalo, NY 14240-1867
IN CANADA: P.O. Box 609, Fort Erie, Ontario L2A 5X3

Not valid for current subscribers to Love Inspired Suspense books.

**Are you a subscriber to Love Inspired Suspense
and want to receive the larger-print edition?
Call 1-800-873-8635 or visit www.ReaderService.com.**

* Terms and prices subject to change without notice. Prices do not include applicable taxes. Sales tax applicable in N.Y. Canadian residents will be charged applicable taxes. Offer not valid in Quebec. This offer is limited to one order per household. All orders subject to credit approval. Credit or debit balances in a customer's account(s) may be offset by any other outstanding balance owed by or to the customer. Please allow 4 to 6 weeks for delivery. Offer available while quantities last.

Your Privacy—The Reader Service is committed to protecting your privacy. Our Privacy Policy is available online at www.ReaderService.com or upon request from the Reader Service.

We make a portion of our mailing list available to reputable third parties that offer products we believe may interest you. If you prefer that we not exchange your name with third parties, or if you wish to clarify or modify your communication preferences, please visit us at www.ReaderService.com/consumerschoice or write to us at Reader Service Preference Service, P.O. Box 9062, Buffalo, NY 14269. Include your complete name and address.

LISUS11B

*Louisa Morgan loves being around children.
So when she has the opportunity to tutor bedridden Ellie,
she's determined to bring joy back into the motherless
girl's world. Can she also help Ellie's father open his
heart again? Read on for a sneak peek of*

THE COWBOY FATHER

*by Linda Ford,
available February 2012 from Love Inspired Historical.*

Why had Louisa thought she could do this job? A bubble of self-pity whispered she was totally useless, but Louisa ignored it. She wasn't useless. She could help Ellie if the child allowed it.

Emmet walked her out, waiting until they were out of earshot to speak. "I sense you and Ellie are not getting along."

"Ellie has lost her freedom. On top of that, everything is new. Familiar things are gone. Her only defense is to exert what little independence she has left. I believe she will soon tire of it and find there are more enjoyable ways to pass the time."

He looked doubtful. Louisa feared he would tell her not to return. But after several seconds' consideration, he sighed heavily. "You're right about one thing. She's lost everything. She can hardly be blamed for feeling out of sorts."

"She hasn't lost everything, though." Her words were quiet, coming from a place full of certainty that Emmet was more than enough for this child. "She has you."

"She'll always have me. As long as I live." He clenched his fists. "And I fully intend to raise her in such a way that even if something happened to me, she would never feel like I was gone. I'd be in her thoughts and in her actions every day."

Peace filled Louisa. "Exactly what my father did."

Their gazes connected, forged a single thought about fathers and daughters…how each needed the other. How sweet the relationship was.

Louisa tipped her head away first. "I'll see you tomorrow."

Emmet nodded. "Until tomorrow then."

She climbed behind the wheel of their automobile and turned toward home. She admired Emmet's devotion to his child. It reminded her of the love her own father had lavished on Louisa and her sisters. Louisa smiled as fond memories of her father filled her thoughts. Ellie was a fortunate child to know such love.

Louisa understands what both father and daughter are going through. Will her compassion help them heal—and form a new family? Find out in
THE COWBOY FATHER
by Linda Ford, available February 14, 2012.

Love Inspired Books celebrates 15 years of inspirational romance in 2012! February puts the spotlight on Love Inspired Historical, with each book celebrating family and the special place it has in our hearts. Be sure to pick up all four Love Inspired Historical stories, available February 14, wherever books are sold.